Ghost
Voyages IV

Ghost Voyages IV

Cartier & Champlain

CORA TAYLOR

COTEAU BOOKS FOR KIDS

© Cora Taylor, 2008.

Edited by Geoffrey Ursell.
Cover painting by Yves Noblet.
Cover and book design by Duncan Campbell.
Typeset by Karen Steadman.
Printed and bound in Canada by Gauvin Press.
Canadian stamps reproduced courtesy Canada Post Corporation.
This book is printed on 100% recycled paper.

FSC

Recycled
Supporting responsible
use of forest resources

Cert no. SGS-COC-2624
www.fsc.org
© 1996 Forest Stewardship Council

Library and Archives Canada Cataloguing in Publication

Taylor, Cora, 1936-
Ghost voyages IV : Champlain and Cartier / Cora Taylor.

Includes bibliographical references.
ISBN 978-1-55050-374-6

1. Champlain, Samuel de, 1567–1635—Juvenile fiction.
2. Cartier, Jacques, 1491–1557—Juvenile fiction.
I. Title. II. Title: Champlain and Cartier.
PS8589.A883G564   2008   C2008-900240-7

10 9 8 7 6 5 4 3 2 1

COTEAU
BOOKS
FOR KIDS

2517 VICTORIA AVE
Regina, Saskatchewan
Canada S4P 0T2

AVAILABLE IN CANADA & THE US FROM
Fitzhenry & Whiteside
195 Allstate Parkway
Markham, ON L3R 4T8

The publisher gratefully acknowledges the financial assistance of the Saskatchewan Arts Board, the Canada Council for the Arts, the Government of Canada through the Book Publishing Industry Development Program (BPIDP), and the City of Regina Arts Commission, for its publishing program.

SASKATCHEWAN
ARTS BOARD

Canada Council
for the Arts

Conseil des Arts
du Canada

Canada

CITY OF REGINA
Regina Arts Commission

To Great-Grandsons
Luc LaPlante,
Taylor Vida,
Aiden Vida and
Michael Hill

and Great-Nephews
Christopher Grieve
Lee Grieve

and, of course, the original Jeremy!

1.

SOMETHING WAS WRONG, BUT JEREMY COULDN'T FIGURE out what it was. Maybe not "wrong" but different. Definitely different. Ever since he'd got back from Toronto that afternoon, his mother had been acting funny. Not funny ha-ha. Different.

He hadn't noticed it at first. No, actually, he had noticed it at the airport when she met him, but he'd been expecting a bit of a change. After all, he'd been gone for a month, visiting his dad. And it was the first time he'd seen his dad since his parents had divorced, when he was four. Seven years was a long time not to see somebody. So it had been awkward for all of them.

He knew his mother had been worried, especially after the business about Dad threatening to sue for custody last year. But that had all worked out, and the visit had been a sort of compromise. All in all, except for a bad moment or two, it had worked out way better than Jeremy had expected. He even liked Pam, his father's new wife. Not that he intended to tell his mother that.

In fact, that had been all he'd been worried about. He had enough friends whose parents were divorced to know that sometimes one parent would use the kid to try to find out how the former partner's new life was going. Especially if one parent had remarried and the other hadn't.

He lay back in bed and closed his eyes. He really was a bit tired. It was only nine o'clock here in Edmonton, but he was still on Toronto time so it felt like eleven o'clock to him.

He was tired, but he couldn't get his brain to stop wondering what was wrong – different – with Mum.

He'd expected a bunch of questions from Mum about Pam. The minute the plane began its descent into Edmonton International Airport he'd started planning what he would say. Nothing. But there were no questions. The "third degree" hadn't happened.

Mum had been happy to see him, lots of hugs and "Jer-Bears," but she hadn't asked any questions except to make sure he'd had a good time. And then she'd seemed rather preoccupied, as if she wasn't really listening to his answers.

He could hear Mum laughing, talking on the phone. She'd been on the phone a very long time. Ever since he'd come into his room to unpack after supper. At least an hour. Strange.

Mum never talked on the phone that long. She was always strict about how long he and Charlie talked. "Fifteen minutes is more than enough for a phone call...you and Charlie see each other every day anyway," she'd say.

The only person she talked and laughed with was Aunt Wendy, but she'd never talk that long. Aunt Wendy was in Prince Albert and that was long distance. Besides, it wasn't her Aunt Wendy voice.

Something was going on. Something different.

He reached over to turn out his light just as Mum knocked on the door. Off the phone at last, he thought.

"Come in!"

His mother opened the door a crack and looked a bit surprised to see that he was already in bed.

"Long phone call..." he started to say and then caught himself.

He couldn't believe it. His mother looked guilty.

"Sorry! I forgot to give this to you," she apologized. "Mr. Matthews dropped it off for you while you were away. Stamps..." She held an envelope out to him as she came into the room. "He said to tell you he was closing the stamp shop for the next two weeks so he wouldn't be needing you Saturday." She turned to leave. "He said he'd phone when he got back."

Jeremy stared as the door closed behind her. That *was* strange. No good night kiss. Not even a "good night."

"Good night," he called.

The door opened and his mother looked even guiltier. "Good night, Jer-Bear!" she said, and quickly shut the door again.

Jeremy shook his head. Something had definitely happened while he was away.

He opened the envelope and spilled out the stamps inside, grateful for the distraction. Ship stamps, of course. Good old Mr. Matthews. Five new ones he didn't have – hadn't even seen before. Maybe he wasn't so sleepy any more. He reached over and dragged his backpack toward him, opened it, and felt for the familiar shape of the old magnifying glass.

2.

MR. MATTHEWS KNEW HE COLLECTED SHIP STAMPS. HE didn't know what Jeremy did with them.

Ever since Jeremy had been given the old ship stamp collection and magnifying glass of his grandad's, he'd done more than just look at the ship stamps. He'd sailed on the ships shown on those stamps. Really. The real ships. Just looking at the ship through the magnifying glass would somehow put him on board.

He sorted through these new stamps. Quite a variety this time. No big explorers, like Captain Cook or John Cabot. He liked the Australian one about the Sydney–Hobart race, and there was a neat triangular one marked *Magyar Posta* – that would be Hungary. One thing stamps had taught him to do was identify other countries. This one had a nice racing boat on it, though he didn't know what the Hungarian words describing it said. He'd have to check it out in the book at the Stamp

5

Shop. There was a stamp with Angus Walters and the *Bluenose,* but he already had that one. He'd sailed on the *Bluenose* quite a bit.

There were a couple of ocean liners: one from *Eire* — that was Ireland — and one from the *Deutsche Demokratische Republik* — that was Germany. Something, it looked like a freighter, from *Republique d'Haiti* too. He'd put them in the book, but he really preferred old sailing ships — more exciting. Especially the ones with explorers. It was fascinating to be on board discovering new places.

He looked at a beautiful big stamp from *Republique Gabonaise.* But it definitely wasn't a picture of the little African country of Gabon. It was Venice, Italy, with a gondola in the foreground and beautiful domed buildings behind. *"Pour Venice* unesco" it said at the top. Mr. Matthews had told him that some small countries issued fancy stamps just for the philately crowd. Stamp collecting was big business and it brought in much needed income for them.

He did prefer travelling on ships or boats from another time, but a gondola ride might just be fun. He'd only stay a little while — it was too early to sleep just yet.

Through the magnifying glass he could see that the boat was quite crowded. By the time he wondered if there was room for him it was too late — he was on board. On board, and standing beside the gondolier, the guy moving and steering the boat. Not a good place to be, but the boat seemed to be full of tourists. Everyone pointing to the beautiful old buildings. They were very impressive, but the smell of the canal wasn't exactly roses.

He ducked as the gondolier's arm came round, almost hitting him. Ducking made him lose his balance and fall onto a man in a bright purple shirt with pink flamingoes on it who was sitting below.

"Watch out!" He turned angrily toward the man next to him. Jeremy scrambled to get away and in the process knocked off the second man's straw hat.

"Hey!" The man made a grab for his hat, poking Jeremy and making him step back – right onto the hat.

Flamingo man saw the crushed hat and started to laugh. Big mistake.

"You'll pay for that!" The second man had picked up his ruined hat and was waving it in the other's face.

The gondolier jumped down to stop the argument. Just then a carillon of bells began from one of the churches along the canal and Jeremy was able to clamber back to where he'd come on board. In the next instant he was back in his room holding the stamp and magnifying glass.

He still wasn't sleepy. He could hear the TV on in the living room. Mum must still be awake. Maybe he could persuade her to join him for a cup of hot chocolate. It would drive away the smell of the canal that still lingered in his nostrils. And something normal like that might get her out of her strange behaviour.

He opened his door and crossed the hall to look into the living room.

"Mum?"

The TV was on and his mother was sitting on the couch. But she wasn't alone.

Jeremy didn't know who the strange man was, but he was sitting awfully close. In fact, he'd had his arm around Mum's shoulders. She jumped guiltily when Jeremy called, and moved over.

"Jeremy!"

No mistaking it. That was her guilty voice. Though maybe it was sounding more upset than guilty now.

"What are you doing up?"

"I was just going to the bathroom." He felt indignant. Since when did he have to make excuses to go pee in his own house? When had this guy come anyway? He hadn't heard the doorbell.

Then Jeremy remembered he'd been causing trouble on a gondola in Venice, listening to the peal of church bells.

His hurt tone must have got through to Mum at least.

"Oh..." she said, "All right."

Jeremy just stood there staring. He couldn't believe it. Wasn't she even going to introduce him?

The staring did it. His mother looked even more flustered. "Ike," she said, looking at the man on the couch as if she was seeing him for the first time, "this is my son, Jeremy! Jeremy this is..." But then she seemed stuck.

Doesn't she even know the guy's last name? Jeremy wondered. He waited.

"...this is Mr. Morton." She paused, fumbling for words again. "Mr. Morton works with me."

Jeremy nodded. He wasn't sure if he was supposed to offer a handshake or what. The Morton guy jumped up and, grinning a big phoney smile, was over in front of him shaking hands as if he was about to sell him a used car or something.

The man had a firm grip, but Jeremy managed to get his hand back in one piece. He mumbled something about it being nice to meet him, pointed down the hall to the bathroom, and fled.

At least now he knew what was "different" about Mum. About everything.

There would definitely be no hot chocolate and cosy chat tonight.

3.

JEREMY LAY IN BED STARING AT THE CEILING. He wished he had somebody to talk to, but it was too late to call Charlie, and anyway Charlie was away. His family always took their holidays in August.

He might have talked to Mr. Matthews at the stamp shop, but that wouldn't be possible. He wouldn't be going to work, since the shop was closed and Mr. Matthews would be out of town, probably visiting his daughter at her cottage at Sylvan Lake.

Even better would be to talk to Aunt Wendy. If the stamp store would be open he could phone from there so Mum wouldn't know. He definitely needed a private talk. When had this Ike character started working at the MacCoshom office? He'd never heard any mention of him before.

He remembered Michael, one of the guys at school, talking about his mother's boyfriend. One minute the man was just dropping by and the next he'd moved in and was bossing Mike around like he owned the place. It wasn't something Jeremy wanted to think about, but his brain wouldn't settle down so he could go to sleep.

He reached over and turned out the light, then tiptoed to his door and pressed his ear against it. He couldn't hear anything. Maybe the Used Car Salesman had gone home. He held his breath and turned the doorknob. There was still a light on in the living room, though he couldn't hear the TV. He couldn't hear talking either, but he knew better than to think that meant the Ike character wasn't there.

Jeremy considered going to the bathroom again, but Mum would hear him and either assume he was spying or decide that he had the scoots or something. Pretending to be sick wasn't a bad idea. Surely that would get rid of the guy.

He sighed and shut the door softly, leaning his forehead against the cool wood. Time enough to do the sick bit later. Best to save it for an emergency, once he found out if the guy was going to be a permanent fixture in his life.

The thought of that nearly turned his stomach. Maybe I am going to be sick for real, he thought. He was feeling queasy, but it could just be a lingering reaction to the smell of the canal and the risk of being bumped overboard into it. That, and the shock of finding out about Mum.

He tiptoed back to bed, crawled in and pulled up the covers.

Lying there in the dark, he knew that sleep wasn't an option. He needed a plan. At least he needed someone to talk to about this. Someone like Aunt Wendy, who knew Mum and would understand and maybe be able to give him some advice. Or somebody who'd experienced something similar. Michael maybe?

Trouble was, Michael hadn't been his friend. Jeremy hadn't even liked him much and the guy had been transferred out of Jeremy's school because he got in trouble all the time. Getting advice from Michael was not an option.

Who else?

He couldn't very well call Dad and Pam. He didn't want to make trouble for Mum.

Funny, wasn't it? When he was in Toronto at Dad's he'd been worried about being taken away from Mum in some stupid custody battle. Now he was probably just in the way of her romance.

He felt sick again. Going from the possibility of being fought over to being the kid nobody wanted wasn't the best feeling in the world.

He'd been tossing and turning, but that last thought had him sitting bolt upright as if lightning had hit the bed. Melanie! The scary girl from Montreal. The one nobody wanted. If only he could talk to her. He lay back and closed his eyes. He was beginning to have a plan.

4.

WHY IS IT, JEREMY WONDERED, THAT PLANS THAT SEEM so brilliant in the middle of the night turn out to be not-so-brilliant – dumb even – in the broad light of day?

He meant to wake up early, maybe have a little time alone with Mum before she left for work. He jumped out of bed the minute he heard her in the kitchen, but by the time he threw on his clothes the door was closing. Hope of her coming back in was dashed when he heard the car start and drive away.

Step one of the not-so-brilliant plan had been to talk to Pam and see if she could find Melanie's phone number. Jeremy figured she'd have gone back to Montreal by now, but Pam would probably be able to get her phone number from her aunt. Maybe there was an email address? Yes, that would be better.

He was sure that he'd be scared to say very much on the phone, but a letter, an email, he could plan. And he didn't have to phone Pam. She'd slipped him her email address as he was leaving. Very thoughtful. Definitely no Wicked Stepmother there. So he wouldn't have a suspicious phone call to explain to his mother when she checked the phone bill.

He looked at the bed, wondering if he might as well just climb back in and do this later. Being up at 7:30 on a summer holiday morning was not his idea of normal living. Too late. He was too wide awake now to go back to sleep. Anyway, he reminded himself, it was 9:30 in Toronto. His head was probably still on Toronto time.

He went to his desk, turned on his computer and started to compose his letter. It was only right to thank Pam and Dad formally for showing him such a good time during his visit, and then he could casually ask about Melanie – if she was still at her aunt's or if she'd gone back, if the aunt knew her email address – stuff like that. He started to type.

Probably, Jeremy thought, as he pressed Send, if he spent this much time rewriting his school assignments his marks would be a lot better. Who knew a simple little email would have to be done over so often? But he wanted to get it just right. A proper thank-you note and a sort of "oh, by the way" asking about Mel. Would Pam (and Dad, if she told him) think he had a thing for Melanie? Probably. But he didn't care.

Now, what to do with the rest of his morning? No more sailing on that gondola stamp, that was definite.

Breakfast, of course. He realized that he was starving. Time to make one of his famous omelettes-with-whatever-was-in-the-fridge. He couldn't wait.

He was just wiping up the last delicious bit with his toast when the phone rang.

Mum, he thought. Maybe she remembered something she wanted to tell him. Maybe she was going to apologize for springing the Ike character on him so suddenly. Maybe... Maybe... More likely, she had remembered that something needed to be taken out of the freezer for supper. It didn't matter; it would be good to talk to her. He picked up the phone and said "Hello?"

"Hey, kiddo!"

It wasn't Mum. It was Aunt Wendy calling from Prince Albert. Even better. Jeremy could feel some of the tension – the Ike stress – draining away.

"I figured you were back in town. How was Toronto?"

Jeremy didn't want to talk about Toronto. He wanted to get right down to what had happened with Mum while he'd been away.

"Good," he said. "It was good."

He stopped. How was he going to bring up the subject of Ike? Had Mum even told Aunt Wendy anything? They were pretty close, sisters and best friends really. There was a big silence on the phone.

Aunt Wendy was laughing. "That good, huh! Did I drag you out of bed or are you just naturally speechless in the morning?"

Still Jeremy couldn't think of how to approach the topic he most wanted to talk about. Toronto seemed years ago. He wanted to talk about now.

"Ummm, Aunt Wendy?" he said. "Do you know what's going on here?"

There. He'd said it. No backing down. If she didn't know anything, that would be that. At least he could tell her and maybe get some advice on how to handle the situation.

This time the long pause came from the other end of the phone.

"Oooh-oh..."

So she knew. And from the tone of her voice, she wasn't all that happy either. Jeremy's heart sank. Aunt Wendy would be the first person to be glad Mum had a boyfriend. She was always telling her: "Get a life, Sandy!"

"Tell me!" he commanded.

"Honestly, kiddo, I don't know much."

Aunt Wendy sounded subdued, not like herself at all. This wasn't making Jeremy feel any better.

"You remember when I decided that your mum needed a break and we went up to Jasper that weekend while you were away?"

Jeremy nodded, then realized Aunt Wendy couldn't see a nod and said, "Uh-huh."

"Well, everything was normal then. We walked, we shopped, we went out for drinks and dinner. A couple of guys wanted to buy us drinks and you'd have thought they were kidnappers." Aunt Wendy was beginning to sound normal again. "Your mum acted like she was about to call the cops!"

Jeremy could feel himself beginning to relax. Just talking to Aunt Wendy was helping, even if he didn't end up knowing more.

"So then I came back to P.A. and we'd talk a couple of times a week...you know...like we always do."

Jeremy knew. Now he was wishing Aunt Wendy would get on with it.

"So what happened?" he asked.

"Last week things changed. I'd phone and she wasn't home in the evening. When I finally got hold of her, she said she'd gone out for drinks with people from work. I thought that was funny. How many years has she worked at that place and she hardly goes to the Christmas party?"

That was true. She used to take him to the kid party but they hadn't gone for quite a while.

"So she hasn't told you about this Ike guy?"

"Ike? Ike Morton?" Aunt Wendy's voice was getting shrill.

She does know something, Jeremy thought. And it isn't good.

"Yeah. The very first night I'm home he's over here." He was about to say "acting like he owned the place" but thought better of it.

"But that's the new guy transferred in from Vancouver. She told me he was driving everybody in the office crazy."

Jeremy leaned his forehead against the wall. The cool wood felt good. He hadn't realized his head was throbbing so much.

"Looks like she's changed her mind," he said.

Aunt Wendy's voice was full of sympathy. "Not good. I wanted her to get out, date a little, but not somebody at work." She seemed to be talking to herself. "Bad idea...office romances."

Jeremy didn't care if he was from work or not. He figured Ike was definitely a bad idea.

"Ooops, sorry kiddo, I've got to run. Listen, I'll get back to you. Hang in there!"

Jeremy hung up the phone. Great. He'd counted on Aunt Wendy sorting things out for him and instead it seemed they were more tangled than ever. It looked like he was on his own.

Would Aunt Wendy phone back? He hoped so.

5.

TROUBLE. TROUBLE FOR HIM AND, IF AUNT WENDY WAS right, trouble for Mum – down the road anyway. Right now she seemed to be happy.

He felt a little guilty. Shouldn't he just let her enjoy this while she could? He didn't want to be the one to rain on her parade, but no way did he want this Ike creature to become a permanent fixture in his life.

He walked into his room. He had a whole day stretching ahead of him. He'd already unpacked and put all his stuff away. He could play one of his computer games but he'd already reached the top levels, so until he got a new one it wasn't much of a challenge.

Maybe someday a virtual reality game could equal the excitement and unpredictability of the stamp-travelling, but for now – his eyes strayed to the stamps spread on his desk – they definitely beat any computer game he'd ever played. He wasn't about to try another of the new stamps. This time he'd stick to something more familiar.

He picked up the old scribbler – *Ships and Boats and Things That Float – Property of Harvey Stark.* Grandad's stamp collection. He'd sailed on quite a few of these but there must be one he'd missed. Slowly, he turned the pages of the book.

He paused at the old ten-cent stamp of the Inuk in his kayak. There was a huge iceberg just behind the man. Jeremy shivered. No. He didn't feel like freezing in the Arctic today. Besides, the kayak was much smaller than the gondola. He'd never used the stamp because he couldn't figure out how an extra body (even an invisible one) would fit in the kayak without scaring the poor Inuk hunter half to death.

There was an old brown one. Issued in 1908 to celebrate Quebec's tercentenary. A twenty-cent stamp showing Cartier's arrival in 1535 with his three vessels. He checked his stamp catalogue. It was one of the first bilingual stamps issued in Canada.

Three ships. It wouldn't hurt to know their names. He picked up his magnifying glass just to see if he could make them out. Otherwise he'd have to google "Cartier," or go out to the living room and check the *Canadian Encyclopedia,* and that felt like work.

Grande Ermine, he read, and that was all he had a chance to do. Too late, he realized he'd picked up the wrong magnifying glass. The old magnifying glass of Grandad's automatically put him on board the ship.

HE COULDN'T SEE A THING, the rain was coming down so hard. In seconds he was soaked. Rain slammed onto the deck until it seemed as if he was wading. At least it wasn't blowing a gale. The ship didn't seem to be tossing about. Nothing to do but head for the hatchway. In spite of the rain, there were sailors on deck and he didn't want to be bumped into.

He'd only taken two or three steps when the sluice of water on the deck made him lose his footing and he crashed down and started to slide towards the railing.

It was sort of like being on the waterslide at West Edmonton Mall, Jeremy thought, but he wasn't going to land in the wave pool – he'd be landing in the Atlantic ocean, and if he did his chances of getting back on the ship were hopeless.

Frantically, he tried to scramble back to where he'd been. He didn't care if one of the sailors saw a suspicious amount of splashing on the deck. The railing seemed awfully close now, almost above him. One final scramble and he slammed into a post, grabbed a coil of rope and hung on for dear life.

For a while he just hung there. The rain was still pouring down, but that didn't seem like such a big problem any more. He could see the hatch doorway. At least he was closer to it now. Slowly, carefully, he stood up and, picking his steps so that if he fell again he'd be close enough to grab something, he made his way carefully toward the hatchway.

At last he reached it and scrambled down the steps out of the downpour.

6.

Jeremy huddled in the corner, waiting for his eyes to adjust to the darkness. His nose didn't need to adjust – the dusty, mouldy smell almost made him sneeze. He hoped if he did none of the sailors working on deck above him would notice. Probably not. They were making enough noise as they hauled on the ropes, adjusting the sails.

At least he was out of the pouring rain. Trouble was, there wasn't much room below deck, and when he saw a sailor rushing toward him, he'd slipped into this little storage space in the hold.

He could see a bit better now. Not much to see. The place was not much bigger than his bedroom closet at home. Wider maybe. Long enough that he could lay down if he wanted to, but a man couldn't. Well maybe some of the sailors he'd seen on deck could. These sixteenth-century guys were pretty short.

He pressed his finger below his nose, trying to hold back the urge to sneeze. It wasn't the dust exactly, more a damp, mouldy smell and something stronger he didn't like.

Something moved in the dark corner opposite him. Something that made scratchy sounds as it slunk out of the shadows.

A rat. Jeremy had never seen a real rat before in his life – what were they called? Norway rats? But he had no doubt about what it was. It was big, way bigger than he'd imagined rats would be, about three times bigger than pet rats. It seemed to Jeremy that it was as big as a jackrabbit or a small dog.

Now he could understand those stories he'd heard about rats in the tenements in New York City eating babies. Seeing this monster rat made him very grateful that Alberta's Rat Patrol kept his province rat free. But he wasn't in Alberta. He was somewhere in the Atlantic Ocean in a tiny room with a huge rat that was crouching a couple of feet away sniffing and snuffling and looking his way. The rat couldn't see him, but it definitely knew somebody was there. Jeremy edged back to the wall, moving toward the door as quietly as he could.

He could hear someone coming down the passageway. He'd have to wait until the sailor went by before he could get away. The footsteps paused outside the door, and he could hear someone muttering.

Jeremy braced himself. If the sailor came in he'd be in trouble. This place was so small he could easily be discovered. Not that the sailor could see him, but he might bump into him and make a grab for him in the dark. He'd be caught. What would these superstitious sailors do with an invisible ghost from the future? Nothing very nice, he was pretty sure.

He held his breath and got ready to make a dash for it out the door. Even if he bumped the sailor, as he surely would, he had a pretty good chance of escaping up the hatch and onto the deck.

But the person didn't come in. The door was pulled shut and Jeremy heard a bolt closing.

His heart sank. He was caught like a rat in a trap. No, he was caught *with* a rat in a trap! How long would it be before anybody needed to come in here to get something? There didn't look to be anything in here except for himself and the rat. He could see a keg or two in the corner, now that his eyes had adjusted. He stared at the rat, wondering what it would do.

He was glad he was wearing shoes. Sometimes on his ship-stamp trips he'd go in pyjamas and bare feet. He could just imagine this monster rat attacking his toes. It made his toes curl in his sneakers just thinking about it.

He had to get out of here. Maybe the bolt wasn't shut tight. He turned and pulled at the door. It was solid. He tugged at it as hard as he could. Nothing. Not even a quiver. He turned back to the rat. It moved back toward the kegs.

It's scared of me! It knows there's something here but it can't see me, so it's scared too. The thought comforted him. A little.

"Boo!" he said, leaning toward the rat and laughing as it jumped backwards so fast it slammed into a keg.

He wasn't worried about anybody hearing him now. His only chance would be to try to slip out if somebody opened the door.

He leaned against the wall shivering in his damp clothes, glad it wasn't colder. Eventually, he guessed, the warmth of his body would dry his shirt. His jeans would take longer.

He shoved his hands in his pockets. His fingers closed around a couple of chewy caramels he'd swiped from the bowl Mum kept in the living room.

The rat poked its nose out from behind the keg and sniffed.

"Good nose!" Jeremy said. He could feel that the candy had melted a bit in his pocket. He threw it, paper and all, toward the rat. He'd expected the toffee to remain invisible the way it had been in his hand, but to his surprise he could see it flying through the air to land in plain sight on the plank floor. This time the rat nearly flipped over backward getting away.

Jeremy laughed. "I think I'm going to call you Templeton, after the rat in *Charlotte's Web*," he decided. "Maybe you can be bribed with food and chew a hole in the door for me."

The rat moved faster than Jeremy could have imagined, grabbed the caramel and retreated back into the safety of its hiding place. Jeremy considered eating the other candy himself but decided to wait in case he got really hungry later on.

He checked his other pocket. A piece of bedraggled Kleenex and something at the very bottom. His knife. The Swiss Army knife Aunt Wendy had given him for Christmas. He'd got it out to pry up a dime that was stuck on some old chewing gum on the bottom of his desk drawer. For some silly reason, having the knife made him feel much better. Now he could defend himself if Templeton attacked. What else could he do? File his nails? Open a bottle if he had one? Carve something? Yes! That was it! He could carve along the side of the door. Maybe if he could get a hole big enough he could slide the bolt back.

Snapping the blade open, he went to work.

7.

It seemed to Jeremy as if he'd been scraping away at the door for hours without making any progress. He had to be very careful not to cut himself. Working with a knife he couldn't see wasn't easy.

He wasn't sure what kind of fastener was on the outside. If it was a latch, all he needed was to get enough space for him to slip the blade of his knife through and lift it up. If it was a bolt type of fastener, then that would be tougher.

Amazing how well fitted the door was. There was hardly enough room for the knife blade to slide through. And the door was thicker than his knife blade, so he'd had to start by trying to cut away enough on this side so that the blade could touch the fastener. So far he wasn't being very successful.

At least now he could clearly see where the fastener was, but he still couldn't reach it with the knife blade.

What kind of wood was this anyway? They must build ships out of the hardest wood around. Definitely not poplar or willow. He'd carved slingshots out of both of those and it only took minutes.

A thin sliver of wood fell to the floor. Jeremy stopped and rubbed his aching fingers. He changed hands and tried to scrape away some of the wood with his left hand. No good.

He wished he was left-handed. He'd noticed that left-handed people, like his friend Charlie, seemed to be able to use both hands. When he'd asked Charlie if he was ambidextrous or what, Charlie'd just laughed and said he figured he was able to use his right hand better because so many things were made for right-handed people that "lefties" just got used to using the other hand more.

Thinking about Charlie made him wish that he was back in his own room in Edmonton in the present, instead of in a galleon on the Atlantic ocean in 1535. Cartier could sail up the St. Lawrence to Montreal without him just fine.

A bit late thinking about that now. He flexed his cramped fingers and went back to work. At least now he was making a bit of progress. There was room to slip the longest blade of his knife in and touch the bolt across the door.

Jeremy held his breath. If he could just lift it up. Gently, carefully, he tried. The bolt didn't move. It was obviously a bolt that slid, not one that lifted. How long it would take him to make a big enough hole to slide it over, he couldn't imagine. He slumped against the door.

Templeton was right at his feet. He was so startled he dropped the knife. Good thing. The rat almost fell over itself trying to get away. And now that he wasn't touching it, the knife, like the caramel, had become visible. If it stayed that way when he picked it up, carving at the door would be much easier.

That didn't exactly cheer him up, but it did take his mind off things for a minute. The rat sure could move when it had to.

He could hear someone scrambling down the hatch ladder. He put his eye to the slit he'd carved. Should he risk calling out so that whoever it was would open the door?

Before he could decide on an answer to that question, the bolt slid back and the door was pushed open, knocking him back against the wall.

There were louder steps now. And the door was slammed completely open, squeezing Jeremy between it and the wall. That hurt! He was pinned there with no chance of escape.

He could only hope that the sailor wouldn't lock the door when he left. He could see the man now, moving in to look around the space. Why didn't he just grab the person he'd been chasing and go?

The sailor was cursing under his breath. "*Fils de cochon!*" was all Jeremy could hear.

Had the other person managed to get out without the sailor noticing? If only the man would let go of the door, Jeremy might be able to slip out from behind it and get by him too. But the sailor held on. Then, still mumbling, he pulled the door shut.

Jeremy held his breath. Hoping. In vain. Disappointment welled up again as he heard the familiar sound of the bolt sliding back. He slumped where he was against the wall, his eyes closed, fighting tears.

Then he heard something – somebody.

Somebody was trying to open the door. From the inside, just as Jeremy had earlier when he'd first realized he was locked in. He opened his eyes. Nobody was there! It was dark in here, but he could see Templeton in the corner, peeking out from behind the keg.

Again, somebody, pulling, trying to open the door. The only explanation was that there was another invisible person in here!

"Harv?" he whispered.

Sometimes when he used the old stamps from the collection he'd inherited from his Grandad he'd run into him as a kid, time travelling just as Jeremy was.

"Jeremy?"

It was the right voice. Relief. Though why he felt so relieved Jeremy couldn't say. After all, they were still trapped.

"Where are you?" Jeremy flailed about with his arms – the only way you could find an invisible person.

"Well…" the voice had moved. "Now I'm sitting on one of those kegs in the corner, so you can find me."

"Ummm…" said Jeremy slowly. "That's Templeton's corner…I hope you're wearing shoes."

"Templeton?" Harv sounded very confused. "You mean there's another stamp time traveller in here?"

"Ummm…Templeton's a rat."

Harv laughed. It was such a cheerful sound Jeremy felt better, even though the situation was still pretty hopeless.

"You really don't like the guy, do you?" Harv was still chuckling. "What does he do…step on your toes and it hurts more if you're not wearing shoes?"

"No, I mean, he's a *real* rat!" Jeremy decided to sacrifice his last caramel in the interest of Harv's toes. He didn't even bother to try to unwrap it, just threw it onto the floor in front of him. The gold-wrapped candy lay there on the floor between Jeremy and the keg. But not for long.

This time Templeton scurried out from behind one of the kegs and stayed in the middle of the floor, the caramel gripped in his yellow teeth as his head turned nervously between the two invisible boys.

There was a scrambling sound from the other corner. Jeremy guessed it was Harv climbing onto the keg he'd been sitting on before.

It was Jeremy's turn to chuckle. The situation might still be hopeless, but with Harv here at least he had a fun companion to share it with.

8.

"So," said Harv from on top of the keg, "how'd you get stuck in here?"

Jeremy laughed. "The same way you did, of course! Somebody coming down the narrow passage. I ducked in here to avoid getting bumped."

There was a minute's silence. *He's going to be as depressed as I am, now that he realizes that we're trapped.*

He should have known better. Harv's voice, when he spoke, had its usual matter-of-fact tone.

"Well, I guess we can be glad it's not as wet in here as it is outside...and that we know the *Grande Ermine* makes it safely to Hochelaga."

Trust Harv to have studied the history before he went on the stamp, Jeremy thought. "You're right. Templeton's probably glad too," he chuckled. "If the ship was sinking, he'd have to leave!" A thought occurred to him. "By the way, Harv, what have you got in your pockets?"

"If I had candy, you'd better bet I'd eat it myself and not give it to that rat!"

By now Templeton had finished the toffee and eaten the wrapper and was looking around nervously.

Harv was taking inventory. "I've got a handkerchief, a couple of allees, the foil wrapper from some chewing gum I was chewing, and which I think I swallowed when that sailor bumped into me and started chasing me down the gangway..."

"Is that all?" Jeremy hadn't thought about it before, but a kid from Grandad's time would carry different stuff than he did.

"That's just one pocket...give me a minute..." One of the marbles flipped through the air and banged on the floor, causing Templeton to do another of his famous backflips and disappear behind the keg Harv wasn't standing on.

"...a button that fell off my shirt yesterday, a couple of Toronto Maple Leaf hockey cards – Syl Apps and Turk Broda – and..." he took a big breath, "my jackknife, of course!"

Jeremy was impressed. The guy carried a lot of stuff. Unfortunately there hadn't been any food on the list, unless they wanted to lick the gum wrapper.

"I'm glad you've got your knife," he said. "I've been trying to whittle the door slot wide enough to slide that latch back, but I dropped my knife just before you and that guy came in..." his voice trailed off.

Where had the knife gone to? It had fallen near his feet and scared Templeton off. He shivered. Good thing he hadn't been holding it when the door slammed him against the wall. People were always getting stabbed that way in the movies.

He began to search. "It should be here on the floor somewhere."

"I can't see it from here," Harv said. Obviously he wasn't coming down off his keg yet. "Maybe the sailor kicked it out when he left."

Jeremy didn't like the idea. He was sure that a modern Swiss Army knife would be very useful to a sixteenth-century sailor, but he really wanted it back.

"Okay, I'll whittle for awhile." Jeremy could hear Harv's boots hit the floor as he jumped off the keg. "You know," Harv's voice was beside him at the door now, "you might check behind those kegs...maybe your friend, the rat, took it. I hear they like shiny things!" Harv was laughing again.

Jeremy didn't care if he was laughing with him or at him. It was nice to have somebody sharing his predicament. Somebody who could still laugh.

9.

Either Harv's knife was sharper than his had been or Harv was a better carver or – Jeremy liked this explanation best – the wood was getting easier to work on. But whatever the reason, progress was being made.

Just on the off chance that Harv was right about Templeton being a knife snatcher, he went over and moved one of the kegs. A trickle of grain of some kind trailed across the floor.

Aha, thought Jeremy, no wonder Templeton's happy here. The other keg felt empty. Templeton stood up, back to the wall, baring his yellow teeth, ready to fight.

"It's okay, Templeton, old ratface," Jeremy said backing away. "Just checking, that's all."

There was no sign of the knife.

Harv was still scraping away at the door. "I wish I hadn't swallowed that gum." Harv seemed to be talking to himself. "We need something sticky to slide that bolt along."

"Can't we just use the knife?" Jeremy wasn't too happy. After all, he'd just wasted two sticky caramels on a rat.

Harv was trying to do just that. The bolt would have some strange scratches on it if anyone ever bothered to check. "We're lucky," Harv said, "at least it's loose and slides easily. I've managed to get it to go a little way. I hope it's the right way. We'll be out of here in a jiffy."

Jeremy wanted to believe him. All he wanted to do was get back to the main mast – which was where he'd come on board the ship – and go home. He wasn't claustrophobic, but this place was getting to him. There was a comforting click, and the door began to swing inward.

Naturally, they both tried to get through the door at the same time. Not being able to see each other was a problem, but they made it and Jeremy pulled the door shut behind him.

"Bye, Templeton," he said as he slid the bolt back.

"There's your knife," said Harv. "How are you going to get that back?"

Jeremy wondered what he meant until he picked the knife up and put it in his pocket. It was visible. He wasn't, and neither were his clothes or any of the other stuff in his pocket, but the knife had been away from him. Obviously, Harv knew that would happen. It hadn't occurred to Jeremy. Now that he thought about it, he'd never dropped anything before, so it hadn't been a problem. It looked as if there was a knife wandering around two feet above the ground. If somebody noticed it, he'd be in trouble.

"When we get up on deck, you'd better hide it somewhere until we've got a clear run to the mast," Harv said.

Now, instead of walking right out on deck when he came up the hatch, Jeremy crawled along, hoping if anyone saw the knife it would just seem to be something sliding across the deck. A couple of men were walking toward him, so he crouched near some coils of rope.

The men were dressed like the French officers, but Jeremy was startled by how much darker they were. They were deep in conversation and it wasn't French.

"That's Dom Agaya and Taignoagny," whispered Harv. "Donnacona's sons...the natives Cartier took back to France to train as interpreters. I guess that was the beginning of the connection the French had with the Algonquin and Huron people who lived along the St. Lawrence."

Jeremy did remember something about that.

"The chief wanted Cartier and his men to help attack their enemies, the Iroquois," Harv added.

"I guess they were impressed by the guns the French had," Jeremy commented. "That would have been a pretty impressive secret weapon."

"The whole thing kind of backfired. For years and years the French would have to contend with attacks from the Five Nations tribes. The gun advantage didn't last long because the English were supplying the

Iroquois with weapons." Harv nudged Jeremy. "Look," he said.

The men were standing by the railing, pointing toward land ahead.

So they weren't in the middle of the Atlantic. It had been raining so hard he hadn't noticed if there was any land to see when he'd come on board. Now he could see steep banks on one side. Were they in the St. Lawrence already?

"It looks as if they recognize the landscape," Harv whispered, pulling Jeremy back. "I'd give anything to be able to understand what they're saying. What must they be feeling, to finally see their homeland again."

Jeremy racked his brain. He did remember something about the men. They had been invited onto the ship, probably thinking they were going for a little ride, and next thing they knew they were in France. For a year.

"Wouldn't you like to be able to warn them?" Harv's voice was pensive. "They're going to see their father and their families again, but they'll be tricked into going back on board the ship with their father. And this time they'll all die in France before Cartier returns for the third voyage."

Jeremy stared. The two men were pointing, their voices raised. Were they excited? Maybe they were even angry. If I were them, I certainly wouldn't trust Cartier and his crew.

"Now!" hissed Harv. "Hurry!"

Jeremy jumped up and ran for the main mast. He didn't even pause to say goodbye to Harv or wonder if any of the sailors noticed a strange object floating across the deck.

Like somebody playing hide-and-seek, he slapped his hand against the mast. And was back at his desk.

He reached in his pocket. His knife was there.

10.

In front of him, the welcome sight of his computer monitor. Flashing something. "You have mail."

Quickly he checked the Inbox. There was one message. From Pam. He couldn't wait to open it.

It was even better than he'd hoped. It began, of course, by telling him how much Pam and Dad had enjoyed having him visit and wondering if he'd like to come again.

He'd expected that. Some sort of general invitation. But this was specific. When was his next holiday? Would he like to come for a long weekend sometime?

That was tempting. And reassuring. At least he was wanted somewhere. He'd think about that later. Quickly he skimmed the bits of news about what she and Dad had been doing since he left.

He was beginning to worry that he'd been so casual asking about Melanie that Pam might have ignored the request. He kept scrolling down until he spotted Melanie's name.

"Your friend Melanie finally went back to Montreal. I'm sure she was bored to death after you left. With nobody to hang out with, she was meeting someone at the movies who her aunt didn't think was a very good influence."

Jeremy was nodding. He remembered the way she'd checked people out when they went to the movie – as if she was looking for someone.

"I'm not even sure which of her parents she's staying with – she goes back and forth quite a bit, as you know. Ghislaine gave me an email address, but wasn't sure if it still worked because Melanie hadn't answered her. Maybe you'll have better luck."

So Melanie was still bouncing around between people. Jeremy wasn't surprised. He copied the email address on a New Message. It might not even get to Mel, so he wasn't going to waste any time trying to write much. Just a "testing" message – "Write me if you get this."

He was about to hit Send, when he decided maybe it needed a bit more. Something to make her curious enough to answer. "I'm in trouble. Please write!" He studied that for a minute, crossed out "I'm in," added another exclamation point after "Trouble" and pressed Send.

He heard a car pull up and stop in front of the house and glanced at his watch. It was nearly five o'clock.

Where had the day gone? Had he really been on the *Grande Ermine* that long?

He jumped up and hurried to the kitchen. He'd cleaned up his brunch mess, but it would have been nice to have surprised Mum by starting supper. He'd noticed she had a chicken casserole in the oven with the timer set to cook it, but he could have set the table or maybe put a couple of potatoes in the microwave to bake. He was just grabbing the cutlery when the front door opened. Funny. She usually came in the back door.

Then he heard voices. No mistaking that jolly, phoney voice.

Jeremy felt like throwing something. Instead, very carefully and deliberately, he finished setting the table. For two. And stood there waiting.

The least he could do was make the Used Car Salesman feel like he was butting in. He braced himself. A real smile for Mum and a "What-are-you-doing-here-again?" look for the ucs would be appropriate.

11.

NORMALLY, JEREMY LOVED MUM'S CHICKEN CASSEROLE. Tonight it seemed to stick in his throat, and when it made it down to his stomach it just lay there like a hunk of lead.

He didn't even try to make conversation, just mumbled replies to the UCS's questions. He stuck to yes and no answers whenever he could, even though his mother was giving him one of her "I'll-talk-to-*you*-later" looks. Obviously, she thought Jeremy should be as smitten with the man's charm as she was.

As soon as he could he excused himself, then thought better of it.

"Do you want me to load the dishwasher?"

His mother smiled. That had been a good move.

"No dear, you just run along and get a start on your homework!"

He looked at her incredulously. Even the UCS seemed shocked.

"It's summer holidays, Mum," he mumbled, puzzled.

She had the grace to look embarrassed. "Ooops!" she said laughing, "force of habit!"

If Jeremy hadn't thought she was losing it before, he was convinced of it now. He went into his room and threw himself on the bed. *Twitterpated.* That was the word. He'd learned it from watching *Bambi* when he was a kid. Mum had explained it meant acting goofy about someone. She'd even sung a song about it. "Everyone is twitterpated in the spring, squirrels go nuts, rabbits sing..." Well, it wasn't spring, but Mum definitely wasn't thinking straight. Obviously – or she wouldn't have had the time of day for that phoney Ike guy.

He probably should have stuck around and made it a threesome. He grinned as he thought of himself beating them to the couch so he could sit in the middle while they watched TV. He'd be one of those old-fashioned chaperones. That might drive the Ike creep away. Jeremy sighed. It might, but it would drive *him* crazy. And somehow, though he hated to admit it, he would probably be the one that was driven away. The Ike character looked to be so full of himself he wouldn't take a hint that he wasn't welcome. And, Jeremy had to admit, his mother certainly didn't seem to be making the man feel unwelcome.

He lay there feeling sorry for himself. Even so, he felt guilty for those feelings. Mum had been on her own for a long time. Jeremy had been her whole life. That and her job and the odd social thing at church. If he was any kind of a person he should be glad she was seeing someone and having some fun. He shouldn't be so selfish. He'd do his best to be nice to the guy. At least until he knew for sure the man was a creep.

Jeremy jumped up and opened his door. And almost bumped into his mother, standing there with a letter in her hand.

"Oh," she said, laughing nervously. "There's a letter for you." She stuck it out at him. "It came the day you got home." She looked embarrassed. "I forgot to give it to you when I gave you the one from Mr. Matthews."

Somehow he wasn't surprised – memory loss was probably just another symptom of being twitterpated. But the letter surprised him. He looked at the envelope, puzzled. "It's from Aunt Wendy," he said frowning. It looked like a card. "Why would she send this...it isn't my birthday?"

"I wondered about that too," his mother said, looking at the envelope, "but I think it's just a 'missing you' or 'welcome home' card or something like that. I think she sent it because of the stamp. Look!"

He hadn't noticed that right away. Mum was right. There was a beautiful ship stamp on it. He grinned, relieved, and squinted to try to read the small print in the dim light of the hall. "Wow, looks like it's Champlain this time."

He turned to go back in his room. "Thanks," he said. He was pretty sure she'd follow him, watch him open his letter and find out what Aunt Wendy had said. She didn't.

"Sandy!" The man's voice was calling from the living room. "Do you want me to start the DVD now?"

Jeremy hesitated. She always read his letters. She'd ask, of course, but he'd never dared refuse. Or even cared one way or the other. This time he would just shut the door when she came in, in case the UCS was curious. None of his business.

But when he turned to let his mother into his room she was gone, and he heard her voice in the living room.

In a way he was glad. He hoped that even though Aunt Wendy wouldn't have written – except to send the stamp for his collection – she might say something about what was going on with Mum. The letter would have been mailed a few days ago. Maybe there was something Aunt Wendy hadn't bothered to tell him this morning because she thought he'd already got the letter.

He wished he'd thought to ask Aunt Wendy about email. She probably had email, but for some strange reason she and Mum had never communicated that way. Probably because of the phone calls. He wondered if Mum had an email address anyway.

He opened the envelope carefully, not wanting to tear the stamp accidentally.

It was a card. The picture was a cross-eyed rabbit looking thoughtful. "Today when I was thinking of our friendship, I realized I wouldn't change it for a million dollars." Cute, Jeremy thought looking inside. "Oh all right! Maybe I would – but I would feel Terribly Guilty about it."

Jeremy laughed, skipped the Xs and Os and read.

"Thought you'd like the stamp for your collection. Why don't you write me sometime?"

He'd always thought Aunt Wendy was the coolest aunt a guy could have, but he hadn't realized she was psychic. There it was. Her email address. This was good. He wouldn't even have to ask Mum.

He couldn't wait to get back online.

12.

HE DIDN'T WRITE MUCH. JUST THANKED HER FOR THE funny card and then, "It was great talking to you today. Thanks for phoning. Sorry you had to hang up so suddenly. I need to know what you think I should do about the Ike character. He came for supper tonight and my mother is totally out of it as far as I can see. She actually sent me to my room to do my homework! What else do you know about him?" He threw in a couple of Xs and Os, pressed Send and sat back.

No mail. Definitely too early to go to bed.

He supposed his earlier idea of going out to the living room to watch the movie and keep an eye on that man was a good one, but he really couldn't bring himself to do it. He could imagine the looks he'd get. Mum would be puzzled, maybe a little annoyed that he was intruding. Ike would probably be really annoyed, but covering it up with that phoney friendly act of his. Probably curious, too. All through supper, when he wasn't asking dumb questions, he'd stared at Jeremy as if he were from some other planet.

Jeremy remembered the two men on Cartier's ship. Dom Agaya and Taignoagny. It must have been horrible for them when they got to France and everybody treated them as if they were zoo animals or something. They'd have been missing home and never knowing when or if they'd get back. The original culture shock. At least he was on his home territory. Even if it didn't feel much like home just now.

He stared at the computer, hoping for the sign that he had mail. He knew it was too early for an answer from Aunt Wendy, but he could hope.

He picked up the envelope and looked at the stamp. "Champlain surveys the East Coast, 1606," he read. He remembered enough from Social Studies to know that Champlain's ship didn't sink, so at least it would be safe to go on board.

It would be nice to know a bit more. He could use the excuse of going into the living room to get the *Canadian Encyclopedia* out of the bookcase, but there was no way his mother would believe he just wanted to know more about the stamp. If it was September he might have made the excuse that he needed it for homework, but looking up history during the summer holidays – no way he could do that without her being suspicious. She'd think he was just checking on her and the Used Car Salesman.

Of course, he was sitting at the computer, so why not google Champlain? He must be losing it not to have thought of that right away.

Too bad there wasn't a chance of meeting the old Harv on board, but the only ship stamps they got to meet on were the old ones – the stamps from the collection that Grandad had travelled on when he was a kid.

He put the new stamp aside. He'd keep it for later. Right now he wanted the comfort of Harv, and the only way he had a chance of that was if he time travelled on the *Grande Ermine*. Maybe Harv was still there or maybe he'd have gone back.

Only one way to find out. At least he didn't have to worry about any interruptions. Mum wasn't likely to come and check up on him – if she even remembered she *had* a son now.

He picked up the old magnifying glass and braced himself for landing on the deck of the sixteenth-century ship.

At least this time it wasn't raining. It could, he realized, even be a different voyage. How many trips had Cartier made? He wished he'd done a little research. The first one, when he'd taken the two natives back to France. So the one he and Harv had just been on was the second, because the men were coming back, and Harv had said that this time they would return to France with Chief Donnacona, Dom Agaya and Taignoagny's father. He remembered now. There was a third voyage, and none of the people Cartier had taken to France had survived to come back home.

He looked around. There didn't seem to be much activity on the deck. In fact, he figured the ship must be anchored and everyone gone ashore.

He was just wondering if he should give up and move back to his landing spot beside the mast when he was bumped, and he heard a familiar laugh.

Jeremy couldn't believe his luck!

"Harv?" he reached out and grabbed an arm. "I was hoping I'd find you again!"

"Me too...but I haven't got much time. My mother's up in arms about the time I spend with the stamp collection. She's gone shopping, so I managed to get away."

Jeremy hated to be reminded of Harv's situation. He knew that eventually Harv would be forbidden to use the stamps.

He remembered visiting Great-Granny Stark in the nursing home in Prince Albert. Her mind was wandering by then and she'd thought Jeremy was her own son.

"You're spending too much time with those stamps," she'd said.

At the time he hadn't understood. He hadn't met the boy who was his grandad yet. Hadn't really known how important the stamp collection would become to him.

"At least you're here." Jeremy looked around. "Although," he said, "I'm not sure where 'here' is...or 'when.'"

"Obviously, the good old St. Lawrence River some-where," Harv replied. "And probably still the second voyage. Of course he did spend the winter of 1535–36. Look at those trees, wouldn't you say the leaves are new?"

It was true. The trees above them on the shore did have that fresh, spring look. And the air was brisk and had the clean, new smell of springtime.

Jeremy took a deep breath. No wonder the air was so fresh and clean. It was nearly five hundred years ago. No pollution! Montreal and Quebec City were just Hochelaga and Stadacona, nothing more than villages. Camps along the river. No factories sending up stinking smoke, just the nice woodsy smell of campfires.

There were fires along the shore that he could see now. People moving about. He could see many birchbark canoes pulled up on shore, and a few wooden boats that must have come from the ship they were standing on. Further along there was a cross and a sort of palisade, a little fort Cartier's men had built, and where they had spent the winter.

"Looks like Cartier and his men are coming back to the ship." Harv was right. Men were boarding the boats and pulling away from shore.

"There won't be as many men to crew the ships back to France," Harv murmured. "Twenty-five of them died of scurvy over the winter, and more would have if Dom Agaya hadn't told them about making a drink out of spruce bark. I think they actually had to scuttle the

Petite Ermine because they didn't have enough crew to sail it."

"Scuttle?" Jeremy was puzzled.

"Sink it on purpose," Harv said.

Dozens, maybe even hundreds of canoes seemed to have appeared from upriver.

"Looks like some kind of farewell send-off party for Cartier," Jeremy said.

Harv sounded impressed. "Wow! Maybe we're going to be in on the departure, when they kidnap the chief."

"Kidnap?" Jeremy didn't like the sound of that. "There are a lot of warriors in those canoes. Looks like Cartier would be making a big mistake."

"Well, maybe kidnap is too strong a word," said Harv. "Wait and see. And let's get out of the way...the men are starting to come aboard."

13.

Harv had grabbed him by the arm and now they were huddled against the upper deck.

Cartier had come onto the *Grande Ermine*. Jeremy could see him waving toward one of the canoes, where a dignified older man sat.

"That will be Donnacona," whispered Harv. "He doesn't look like he's going to come aboard."

That was good news to Jeremy. Maybe Harv had his history wrong. Maybe they didn't come. He could see Dom Agaya and Taignoagny sitting with their father. They were frowning and arguing with him. Good for them!

Now Cartier's men brought out some very impressive gifts and were holding them up.

Reluctantly, Donnacona rose and began to climb aboard the ship.

Jeremy wanted to run forward and shove him back – off the ship, into the water. "You'll never see your home again!" he wanted to warn them. But he knew now that Harv was right and he couldn't prevent what was going to happen from happening any more than he could have saved Captain Cook's life.

Sure enough, the minute Donnacona and his sons, who had followed him, were on board the ship, Cartier's men seized them.

In an instant a great cry rose from the people in the canoes and several hundred who had gathered on shore. The ululating sound of hundreds of voices seemed to swell, echoing across the river.

"Maybe we should get back to the mast and get out of here," Jeremy whispered, tugging at Harv's arm.

"I've got to go, but you can stay," Harv whispered. "It'll be okay. Cartier persuades Donnacona that as king of Canada he should go to meet the king of France."

There was some earnest conversation going on. Obviously Taignoagny, who was doing the translation, was trying to persuade his father that this was not a good idea. But the older man was busy trying on the fancy French clothes he'd been given and seemed to have decided that he would go.

Jeremy was just about to speak to Harv when he heard him say, "See you," and realized Harv had left.

He had to grin at that. One thing he and Harv had never done was "see" each other. It felt like he knew Harv so well, but he had no idea what he looked like. It hadn't occurred to him before but he began to wonder what Grandad had looked like as a kid. Maybe he'd get Mum to dig out some of the old family albums so he could see for himself.

He watched while Donnacona moved to the railing facing the shore and started a long speech. Obviously he was telling his people that he was going and appointing someone to act as chief while he was away.

Time to go, Jeremy thought. But one more thing to do before he did. He moved to the other side of the ship, leaned over the railing and took another deep breath. The mixture of pine and cedar and fresh new leaves was one he'd remember next time the smell of exhaust fumes in Edmonton or Refinery Row in Sherwood Park got to him. He was savouring the clean, pure scent as he stepped up to the mast.

Back home, he looked down at the stamp. Maybe he'd travel on it again, even if it was just because he hoped to run into Harv. Somehow the connection made him feel less alone.

One of the unwritten rules he and Harv followed was that they didn't discuss the problems they had back home in their own times. Well, Harv had told him that his mother was going to crack down on his time with the stamps, but that was because it affected whether they would see each other again. And Jeremy had told Harv how valuable the old stamps might one day become. That had worked out beautifully. Grandad had collected the stamps Jeremy told him would eventually be valuable. That money had helped a lot.

So maybe the unwritten rule wasn't really important. Maybe he could talk to Harv about his Ike problem. Not much Harv could do, except he was a sensible guy, and at least it would be someone to talk to. It made Jeremy feel better just thinking about it.

He looked over to his desk. The light on his computer was flashing. Maybe Aunt Wendy had replied to his email. Even if she didn't have any new information about the Used Car Salesman, he hoped she'd have some advice on how to handle the situation.

But the email wasn't from Aunt Wendy.

He'd almost forgotten that he'd written to Melanie.

14.

"HI WOTS THE TROUBLE U PREGNANT ROFL"

Melanie obviously didn't believe in punctuation or capitals. Jeremy grinned. Or in writing very much.

He hit Reply and started to type.

"Not preg. Mum has boyfriend who seems total jerk. Any suggestions? And can we Instant Message?" He hit Send and sat back.

Staring at the computer screen didn't seem to be useful. He decided to google Champlain. Try to find out what the 1606 trip had been all about. The small sailing vessel on the stamp didn't look like it would have crossed the Atlantic. Though, even as Jeremy thought that, he remembered how tiny Captain Cook's *Endeavour* had been. Not even as long as some of the Maori war canoes.

Funny, he thought, as he sat back to wait for the information to show. There must have been earlier Champlain stamps. An important explorer like that.

He reached over to his bookshelf for his *Catalogue of Canadian Stamps*. The tercentenary stamps that were issued at the same time as the Cartier stamp had two Champlain stamps, but neither of them showed ships. One was for five cents, showing his "habitation" – a very impressive house. The other was entitled "Champlain's departure," but just showed people gathered on the shore – no ships, a couple of canoes.

The stuff that came up on Champlain wasn't too helpful. Who knew there were so many places, colleges and things named after him? Jeremy had to go through pages of stuff before he finally got a little information on Champlain, Samuel de.

Jeremy remembered hearing Champlain called the "Father of New France," but this web page called him "Father of Canada." He had spent most of his life in Quebec City and died there in 1635. In the meantime, he made twenty trips back and forth between France and Canada.

Wow, thought Jeremy. That's a lot of travel for those days! Mostly, he supposed, it would be negotiating things with the king and other powerful people in France about starting the new colony.

Here was something: "Champlain came over with the de Monts expedition in 1605 and spent the first three winters in Acadia." That was Nova Scotia, wasn't it? So in 1606 he wouldn't have been in Quebec at all. Someplace called Port Royal in Nova Scotia. Well, the stamp said "Champlain explores the East Coast in 1606," and the

Maritimes were the East Coast. So the ship on the stamp wasn't about the St. Lawrence part of his life. Interesting.

He reached for the magnifying glass. He was just about to put it to his eye when he noticed the flashing light.

Melanie?

Quickly he clicked on New Mail.

"is that all your on about – mums boyfriend – not sure how to get rid of him – i got rid of a couple by saying they were coming on to me but then she didn believe me when one really did guess that won't work for you – wots the creep done anyway m"

What had "the creep" done? Nothing really, Jeremy had to admit. Except hang around. Keeping him from having a hot chocolate talk with Mum his first night home.

He'd just started to type his reply to Mel when there was a knock on the door and his mother stuck her head in, a big smile on her face.

"Ike wondered if you wanted to go out for ice cream with us?"

Jeremy just sat there. Ice cream? What sort of deal was this? He started to shake his head no and then decided it would look bad if he didn't go along with this.

"Sure," he said, forcing a smile. "I'll be right there."

His mother gave him a big happy smile as she left. It made him feel a bit guilty. Mum seemed so pleased about it all.

"Not much so far," he typed quickly. "Got to go – he's taking us out for ice cream. Some evil plan no doubt. Jer" He pressed Send, grabbed his jacket off the back of his chair, and went to the front door, wondering what this was all about.

He followed Ike and Mum down the front sidewalk to Ike's car, waited while he opened the passenger door and his mother settled herself inside. Jeremy quickly climbed into the back seat.

The car was a late model – a sporty looking Audi. It smelled brand new. Jeremy couldn't help being impressed.

It must have shown, because as Ike was doing up his seat belt he looked back at Jeremy and said, "It's leased."

Jeremy was amazed. Ike didn't need to tell him that. He could have just gone ahead and let him believe he owned the car. Being honest about something like that didn't fit the fast-talking, used-car-salesman/con-man image he had of the guy.

He was glad that nobody said anything to him on the way. Ike and Mum were talking about work, and Jeremy wasn't listening anyway. He was too busy trying to sort out his feelings.

What if the guy was really nice and he'd be good to Mum and she wouldn't have to worry about money any more, or about Car-la-la? That was what she called their old Dodge, which was always threatening to break down, and frequently did.

No! That was just too much speculation for him to handle right now. He wondered where they were going. McDonald's? But no, they'd already passed a couple. They were heading down ninety-seventh, into city centre.

"Turn left," his mother was saying.

Of course, Jeremy thought. The man was new to Edmonton. Great. She was directing him to Little Italy. They were going for gelato. Way to go, Mum! His mouth was starting to water.

They hadn't been here for ages, but it had been one of their special places for celebrating things. Like the rare occasion when he got an A on his report card or Mum got a raise.

He wasn't sure Ike was worth celebrating, but any excuse would do. He loved licorice gelato. He would even put up with some phoney conversation-making questions from Ike, like if he was looking forward to school starting in September.

He was glad his mother turned down the booth. He didn't want to sit opposite Ike and he sure as anything didn't want to sit beside him. At the little round table he could edge his chair closer to Mum.

"So," it was the used car salesman jolly voice again. "Are you looking forward to getting back to school?"

Groaning inwardly, Jeremy put on the best half grin he could manage. "It'll be okay, I guess."

"Guess you'll be glad to see all your friends anyway..." The man obviously wasn't going to give up. "Especially the girls!"

Was the man actually leering at him? Yuck!

Luckily, his mother and the waitress came to his rescue. True to form, Mum needed to know if there were any new flavours other than the long list on the wall behind the counter. And she'd want to discuss every possible combination. Even though, as Jeremy very well knew, she would end up ordering lemon. She always did.

He was grateful, though, that Ike wasn't aware of this and got involved in the flavour discussion.

Maybe, he thought, when the waitress finally left to get their ice cream, he should kick into the conversation. Anything would be better than getting back on the school topic. Besides, it would make Mum happy if he looked like he was interested in talking to Ike.

"So," he said, taking a deep breath. "How do you like Edmonton?"

He couldn't help but notice the surprised look on his mother's face. She wasn't used to Jeremy starting conversations with people he hardly knew. But, he realized, it was a look of pleased surprise, so he guessed he'd done the right thing.

Ike looked surprised too, but he went into his happy salesman voice. "Oh, I'm enjoying it here very much!" He had a huge grin on his face as he reached over and took Jeremy's mother's hand. "I had no idea things in Edmonton were sooo lovely!"

Jeremy felt like tossing his gelato. Except it was just arriving, so at least he could put his head down and eat.

That would teach him to try to make conversation with the creep. He couldn't even bear to look at his mother. She was sitting there with a silly, happy look on her face.

It was worse than he'd thought.

15.

Jeremy excused himself to use the washroom as soon as he finished his gelato. He didn't have to go, but he wanted to give Mum and Ike time to finish theirs, and he didn't want to talk to them. He didn't want to watch them talk. And he sure didn't want to see the dopey looks on his mother's face.

Smart move. Ike had just finished paying the bill when he returned, so all he had to do was follow them out to the car.

He couldn't wait to get out of the car at home, though he caught his mother's warning look and gave Ike a sort of smile and said, "Thanks for the ice cream!" before he went up the walk.

He unlocked the front door and went in. He wasn't about to hang around. He didn't figure he'd be appreciated.

He went straight to his room. The New Mail light was flashing but it wasn't Mel.

"Hey kiddo!" Aunt Wendy had written. "Been trying to phone you guys tonight. Don't tell me you are dating the guy too! What's up? Keep me posted on my sister's romance. Your Good Old Aunt W."

Jeremy figured he had time to answer if he was quick about it. No way he wanted Mum coming in and reading this over his shoulder.

"He took us for ice cream – gelato was good – watching Mum goo-goo over the Ike was not. What should I do? Help! Your Good Young Nephew J"

He pressed Send just as he heard the front door open. Should he wait for Mum to come in, or stick his head out of the bedroom and make sure she was alone? He did, and she was. But she still had the goober look on her face.

"Good night!" he said. No way did he want to talk about the evening.

But it was obvious his mother did. "Want some hot chocolate?" she was asking.

He was saved by the phone ringing.

"I'll get it!" his mother rushed down the hall to her bedroom.

Did she think the Ike character was calling already?

"Oh hello, Wendy." She did sound a tad disappointed.

Jeremy closed the door. He wouldn't risk listening on the hall phone. He was off the hook for a heart-to-heart talk with his mother about the merits of Ike. As far as he was concerned, that could be postponed indefinitely.

Suddenly he was very tired.

16.

He slept in. Didn't even try to wake up before Mum left.

While he was throwing things in his omelette bowl, he did something he hadn't done for a long time. He mentally made himself a Good Things/Bad Things list.

He started with the Bad Things list.

1. Ike
2. Not knowing What to Do About Ike
3. Mum regarding Ike

He wracked his brain, but there didn't seem to be anything else for the Bad Things list. He smiled as he crumbled some cheese into the egg mixture: Did having so few Bad Things count as a Good Thing?

Good Things list.

1. He had people (Mel and Aunt Wendy) to talk to about his trouble even if they hadn't suggested anything useful yet.
2. Charlie would be back from his holidays this week, so he'd have somebody to hang out with. And talk to.
3. He had the stamps to escape on.
4. He was about to eat another omelette masterpiece.

Whenever he made the lists, the trick was to make the Good list longer than the Bad one.

He hadn't even tried to fudge the results either, he thought, as he buttered his toast and sat down at the table with his omelette. First mouthful was the taste-tester.

Yum. He'd chopped up a couple of slices of ham, some onion, some hot pickles and cheese, and some of Mum's special herb mix. The onions had a bit of a crunch, the hot pickles gave it zip, the cheese had melted its way through everything, and the ham and egg got along just right. Yes, he smiled as he surveyed his plate, definitely A Good Thing!

And afterward, he'd finally try that Champlain stamp.

There was one disappointing thing about the stamp, of course. It wasn't one of the old Grandad stamps. But he might meet the other Harv. Because any stamp that

Jeremy added to the collection would eventually end up being owned by his future grandson. Another time traveller on the stamps.

Weird, being able to know both your grandfather and your grandson and all of you being the same age. And not being able to tell either of them.

He'd thought of it several times with the original Harv, but even though they'd met so many times and knew they came from years apart, he'd never figured out a way or dared to tell him.

The new Harv was different. Jeremy doubted that the kid ever thought about anything serious. He accepted that Jeremy was a time traveller from another time but never questioned why they used the same stamps. Of course, he didn't know the business of why his name was Harvey. If it hadn't been for that, and the stamps, Jeremy might not have figured it out himself, even though he had the letter from Grandad before he died, talking about using the "magic" of the stamps.

What was it that letter had said? Something about being in trouble and "needing" the stamps? Funny, he hadn't thought about the letter and those words for a long time.

Well, he felt like he was in trouble now, and he guessed the stamps helped a little. Even if it was only to remind himself that he wasn't as badly off as Dom Agaya and Taignoagny.

Maybe it was just the distraction. Escaping via the stamps was just as exciting as playing video games, and you got used to those after a while and knew what to expect. He'd never expected to land with Cabot in 1497. Or meet friends, or famous people like Captain Cook.

He smiled. Maybe it wasn't so bad after all. Back at his desk he picked up Grandad's old magnifying glass, settled back and looked at Champlain's ship.

17.

This time, he landed at the stern of the boat, which was probably a good thing since there were so many people on board. The boat wasn't that large, though it did have two sails. Luckily, too, all the people were standing around the prow, so he needn't be afraid of bumping anyone.

Something squirmed under his leg. He jumped aside. Not another rat? Not up here in the open. Nothing there. Either the rat had taken off in a hurry or...

"Jeremy?" The whispered voice was very close.

He might have known. "Harv?... Hey!" He couldn't help grinning. It was always fun to have a companion, and he hadn't been with this new Harv since that awful time when Captain Cook was killed and he'd barely managed to save the kid. It would be nice to spend some time together when their lives weren't in danger.

The weather was beautiful; there was just enough wind to take them along the coast. The crew was busy and not likely to be bumping into them, especially if they stayed perched up here. And they were just inches away from where they had to be if they wanted to get back home.

"So how are things in 2056?"

"Aaah, not so good," Harv said. "I was hoping to spend some time visiting my Uncle Joshua...he's living on the moon colony? But Mum says my marks aren't good enough."

"Get out!" Jeremy couldn't help but sound shocked. It wasn't the idea of a colony on the moon either. He was certainly disappointed. "You mean you've still got tests at school and stuff like that!"

"School? Nope, just the really bad kids go there..."

"Like jail?"

"Yeah...sort of..."

Jeremy could tell Harv was having a problem with this.

"My teachers are on the computer, so I work at home. I have to put in a certain number of hours...and get everything done or I'm reported."

"And then?" Jeremy prompted. It was interesting finding out what life was like in the future. Some things changed so much, like having an uncle living on the moon.

"First your parents yell a lot, and if you don't smarten up then you have to go to school, where they make sure you work. But even at home there are tests and marks."

Some things never change, Jeremy thought. Not only that. Obviously the stamp magic was working for Harv's problems too.

"Hey!" Harv was poking him. "What kind of flag is that?"

Although he couldn't see Harv's finger, Jeremy figured he'd be pointing up at the blue and white flag flying from the top of the mast.

"That's the old French flag. What's France's flag like now?...I mean in your time."

Harv sounded puzzled. "You mean the Euro flag? I don't think France has a flag any more."

Jeremy hadn't noticed one of the crew moving back toward them until he was right there, staring in their direction with a horrified look on his face.

The man was so close now that he could clearly see a scar that seemed to wind its way through his unkempt beard. Worse than that, where Jeremy sat was at eye level with the man's waistline. So he had a very clear view of an old pistol type of gun shoved into the sash wrapped around his waist. The gun the man was now reaching for.

Harv was babbling on, oblivious to the threat right in front of him. "Some of the countries were pretty upset when that..."

Jeremy didn't let him finish. He grabbed Harv's arm and yanked him over as he ducked down just before the "click," followed closely by the flash of powder as the gun seemed to explode in front of them.

18.

THEY'D FALLEN DOWN ONTO BALES OF SOME KIND. Crashed down, really. Luckily, the report of the gun, and the cries of the men who were now dashing back to see if they were being attacked, covered up the noise of their fall and the noise they were now making scrambling to get out of the way.

Harv was trying to shake Jeremy's hand loose from his arm, but Jeremy wasn't about to let go. If they got separated, who knew what might happen to Harv?

"Gardez!" somebody in the front of the boat was yelling.

He and Harv were squished against each other now, pressed against the side of the boat. They were out of range of the wild-eyed man with the gun, who was now trying to explain why he'd fired at nobody.

Jeremy couldn't understand the French he was talking, but he could tell by the looks on the other sailors' faces that they were no longer alarmed by some threat to the ship, and were beginning to think the man had fired for nothing.

"...*es fou*," one of the men mumbled as the others began to make their way back to their places.

Jeremy relaxed a little. He knew enough French to know that meant the other sailor thought the man with the gun was crazy. He'd probably told the men he'd heard voices. Now all he and Harv had to do was wait until the man left.

Except when he moved a bit he realized Harv wasn't beside him anymore. Where had he gone? It wasn't safe – the man who'd heard them talking was still there, poking around in the stern of the ship where he and Harv had been sitting. Surely Harv hadn't climbed back up there?

Suddenly the man jumped, and spun around as if somebody had poked him in the back.

Jeremy's heart sank. He had no doubt that somebody really had poked the guy, and he had no doubt about who it was. Harv's idea of a prank.

The sailor was waving his gun wildly in all directions, although luckily he wasn't firing. There was nothing Jeremy could do. He didn't dare go over and try to catch Harv again. Who knew where he'd be now? And, although he was pretty sure those old guns could only fire one shot before being reloaded, he wasn't about to risk getting in the way, just in case he was wrong.

Right now all he wanted to do was get back to the place in the stern where he'd come on board, so that he could get back home. This time he'd even leave Harv to his fate. The kid was just too much of a daredevil to be a safe travelling companion.

A couple of men had come back to see what was happening, making his chances of getting away even more risky.

He felt somebody squeeze in beside him. Harv was back. Jeremy wasn't sure whether he was happy about that or not. No telling what the dude would do next.

"Pretty good trick..." Harv was chuckling close to him. "I really had that sailor going, didn't I?"

Jeremy grabbed Harv's arm. This time he wasn't going to let go. The sailors were now yelling at their shipmate, so he figured it would be safe to speak to Harv.

"Are you out of your mind?" he said halfway between a whisper and a growl. "If that guy catches you, being invisible won't save you from being shot...or something worse..."

Harv didn't say anything, and Jeremy was pretty sure that he wouldn't have let caution over the risk of being heard stop him. He hoped Harv was actually thinking it over.

"All he has to do is grab an arm or leg. Invisible or not, you could be caught. They could tie you up." Jeremy wracked his brain for something awful. "You could be...you could be keelhauled!"

"Keelhauled?"

Jeremy might have known the future Harv wouldn't know that word. He'd have to explain. It had been one of the things he learned when he did research on the *Nonsuch*. He wouldn't even have to exaggerate to scare Harv. The truth was bad enough.

"It was the worst punishment they could give a sailor in the old days. Worse than being whipped until the man collapsed. Hardly anybody survived."

"Yeah?" Harv didn't sound too impressed. "So what did they do?"

"They'd tie a rope around the guy and drag him under the ship from one side to the other. By the time he came up on the other side he was bleeding pretty bad from all the barnacles on the keel...if he hadn't drowned." Jeremy waited for this to sink in. He hoped Harv was imagining what it would feel like. "Usually the guy was more dead than alive when they finally pulled him out of the sea and dragged him back on deck."

"Wow...talk about inhumane punishment. It should have been illegal!"

Jeremy was glad Harv seemed to be giving things some serious thought at last. "Those ships would be gone for years sometimes. In those days the captain was the only law."

"I don't think they'd do that here...would they?" Harv's tone seemed uncertain.

Jeremy didn't think so either, but he wasn't about to say anything. Let Harv worry a bit.

The sailors had taken their companion and were walking him back toward the prow of the ship. They were met by a handsome man with a long straight nose, who seemed to be one of the men in charge.

Champlain! Jeremy thought excitedly. Could that be him? He didn't look much like the portrait on the web page. His grip on Harv tightened. He wasn't about to have the kid running loose, poking Champlain and causing any more trouble.

There were some excited explanations. The sailor who'd fired the shot and then been poked by Harv seemed to realize that his story wasn't making much of an impression on anyone. Champlain shook his head, then gestured to the men.

Was he ordering them to search the ship? Jeremy decided he wasn't going to wait and see if there'd be more investigation. This ship wasn't that big and there were only so many places to hide.

"We'd better be quick," he whispered, "and get back to where we came aboard before they start poking around back there, or post a guard or something."

Harv seemed to understand, and the two of them moved quickly, scrambling up. Jeremy arrived first. Before he even thought to say goodbye he was back in his bedroom holding the stamp in one hand and the magnifying glass in the other.

He could only hope that Harv was safely back home where he belonged too.

19.

WHY WAS IT, JEREMY WONDERED, THAT TIME TRAVELLING with the new Harv always turned out to more complicated than it should be? Of course, the kid didn't seem to know any history, which could add to your problems when you were travelling back in it.

As Charlie's dad was always saying, "If you don't study history, you end up repeating it." Maybe those weren't his exact words, but he said something like that. Of course, he used to teach history. And he was always complaining that students weren't getting enough of it any more.

Maybe he was right. The old Harv, Grandad as a kid, knew a lot more than Jeremy did, but Jeremy was a raging genius compared to the new Harv in 2056.

Jeremy wasn't sure that studying history helped. People didn't seem to learn lessons from it. Look at all the bloodshed caused by the French supplying the Hurons and Algonquins with guns, while the English supplied the Iroquois and Mohawks. That sort of thing was still going on today all over the world. Big countries supplying arms, while the poor people in third world countries got killed.

But it wasn't just not knowing history that made the new Harv a risky travelling companion. The kid just didn't seem to recognize danger. Not that he was terribly brave. Jeremy was pretty sure that being brave meant you knew you were in a dangerous situation and you did something anyway. It was more that he took risks without thinking. Jeremy hoped he'd made it off the ship safely.

It had been quite a morning. Jeremy glanced at the clock by his bed. Morning? It was one o'clock in the afternoon. He still had a few hours before Mum got home.

Now he could earn some big-time brownie points and do something about supper. He'd noticed Mum had left out meat of some kind to thaw when he'd been poking around in the fridge that morning. Maybe he could get a couple of potatoes ready to nuke.

There were, he saw to his regret, more than two chops thawing. Four. He knew better than to think she was inviting two other people. The other two chops were obviously for Ike. He cancelled plans for doing anything to help, stomped back to his room and plopped down in front of his computer.

The Instant Message light was flashing. Good. Maybe Mel was coming up with some advice.

"so did he poison ur ice creme or wot?"

"No and I still need advice about how to get rid of him," he typed and sent.

Poison the ice cream? No, but he could dump a lot of cayenne on his pork chops. Jeremy liked the idea – not that he'd do it. With his luck, he'd probably end up eating that one himself.

"very tricky must convince mother he is bad while making it look u like him"

Thanks Mel, Jeremy thought, how am I supposed to do that?

"important she must think u want him around gotta go bye"

That wasn't much use. Jeremy typed, "Bye. Get back to me when you can." He wondered if she'd even hung around to get his reply.

He could pretend that he liked the guy, but wouldn't that make Mum want Ike around even more? If she thought Jeremy was going to have a stepfather he liked? Jeremy shuddered. Stepfather. That was the first time he'd let himself think of *that* possibility.

He wondered why he hadn't had any message from Aunt Wendy. Mum hadn't said anything about the phone call. It wouldn't hurt to email her again. If she'd found out anything, she should at least share it. Unless – Jeremy hated the thought – she had bad news – so bad she didn't want to tell him. Maybe, he thought grimly, the situation was even worse than he imagined.

What could be worse than suddenly having a potential stepfather thrust into his life in less than four days?

It just wasn't like his mother. She of the "Let's talk it over," "check it out," "take our time" over minor stuff like whether to increase the number of channels they got on cable TV. Surely she wouldn't rush into something big? It was totally out of character. That consoled Jeremy for a little while – until he remembered the dopey smiles and the "Let's have a talk." Then he felt grim again. The whole situation was out of character for his mother. Who knew what she would do?

For the first time, he wondered what it had been like when she got married to Dad. Had she rushed into that? He didn't know anything about their getting together, engagement or anything. She'd never talked about that time of her life. And, by the time Jeremy was old enough to ask questions, she'd been so bitter about the divorce that she wouldn't talk about his dad at all.

He decided that he'd ask Aunt Wendy again, and if he didn't hear from her by tomorrow he'd phone.

That consoled him a little. Not enough.

He picked up the Champlain stamp again. Had Harv managed to get off the boat? At least wondering about that took his mind off his other problems. And this was something he might be able to find out about. He reached for the magnifying glass and quickly put it down. First he'd do a little research.

The *Canadian Encyclopedia* called Champlain "Father

of New France" and it praised his abilities as a cartographer. That was what the 1606 voyage was all about. Making maps. There were four maps in the encyclopedia showing his travels, and one showed his trip in 1606. Champlain had made charts of the coastline as far south as Cape Cod.

The encyclopedia entry also said, "There is no authentic portrait of Champlain." Jeremy shrugged. He'd been warned that you couldn't always trust information you found on the Internet – after all, anybody could make a web page and put stuff online.

Back in his room, he used the magnifying glass to look at Champlain's stamp.

Canada 51

20.

THIS TIME THE SHIP WAS ANCHORED IN A BEAUTIFUL bay. The trees along the shore were vivid with autumn colours and he recognized the crispness of fall in the air. It seemed as if the sun was just over the treetops – the start of a lovely day.

It looked like quite a big settlement here. There were fields of ripened corn, and campfires here and there along the shore. There was a large cross too. Obviously the crew had been ashore. Jeremy remembered the cross Cartier had set up along the St. Lawrence. He supposed that it was not just to establish a sign of their religion, but to serve as a landmark. Closer to the water's edge he could make out a sort of tent.

What was happening? It seemed nearly everyone was on deck. They were facing the land, talking excitedly. Jeremy moved over to get a better look.

This time he knew the warm thing he bumped into wasn't a rat.

"Harv?"

He recognized the chuckle. "Jeremy! Am I ever glad you came!" Harv was speaking fast but softly. "Lots of excitement! Last night the natives moved their wigwams and sent all the women and children away into the forest. So the captain, his name is Poutrincourt, ordered all the men to come back aboard the ship...but some didn't obey. Now it looks as though they were killed."

Harv was right. Jeremy could see bodies lying near the tent. One man had died at the water trying to get back to the boat; he could see arrows in his back. This was shocking. Almost as shocking as the fact that Harv suddenly seemed to know an awful lot. Had he started studying history all of a sudden?

"How do you know all that?"

"I brought my translator."

"Translator?" This was amazing. Jeremy was impressed. "You mean you've dragged somebody here who understands the Old French these men are speaking?"

Harv laughed. "No...it's not a person! It's a little machine. Like a recorder, or a phone. I just set it for the language...and then the time...sixteenth century seems to work. Here! You try it. Just hold it to your ear. I've got it tuned to pick up what they are saying."

There was a fair bit of fumbling trying to find each other's invisible hands but finally the item was in Jeremy's hand. Harv was right. It was the size of a cellphone. He wasn't sure how Harv had managed to set it — maybe he'd done it at home before he and the translator became invisible. Jeremy held it to his ear. Before, he could barely hear the men talking, but obviously Harv had figured out the volume very well. Suddenly he could hear clearly. And in English.

"Prepare to go ashore and bury the men." This man must be the captain; his orders were being promptly obeyed.

"*Arquebusiers!* Musketeers!" Someone else was calling. "Take arms."

Jeremy shook his head. This machine was amazing. He moved forward, watching as a group of men quickly disappeared over the rail, climbing down to the ship's boats below.

"Come on!" Harv was right beside him. "Let's see if we can get onto one of those boats."

Here we go again! Jeremy thought. It'll be Captain Cook all over again, and this time one of us may get hit.

"No way!" How was he going to persuade Harv to stay put. "Look!" He knew Harv couldn't see where he was pointing but it was pretty obvious. From every part of the forest men were appearing. And if the noise they were making wasn't war cries, Jeremy didn't know what was. "We'd better stay out of the way. Besides, we've got a ringside view from here...and we won't get shot by either side."

Harv sounded reluctant, but to Jeremy's great relief he gave in. "Okay! It looks like there's a couple of hundred of those guys...and more coming out of the woods."

The first of the boats had reached shore and the men with the funny old muskets had lined up on the beach, firing, but by then the attackers had disappeared into the forest.

As Jeremy watched, more boats were landing and men were wading ashore. The captain and the man he thought was Champlain were there. Quickly, the men had moved to gather up the bodies. It seemed four men had been killed. Graves were dug at the foot of the cross, and what was obviously a funeral service was taking place. The voices were out of range of the translator now. All Jeremy could hear was a murmur, almost drowned out by the shrieks of the men lurking out of sight in the forest.

"Harv!" Jeremy had a sudden thought. This would be his only chance. "Would you stand watch for me in case one of those men goes below?"

Three men had stayed on board. They were standing at the railing intent on what was taking place on shore, but Jeremy didn't want to take any chances. "I want to go down to the captain's quarters, or chart room...or whatever they've got on this boat...and see if I can get a look at Champlain's maps."

To his relief Harv agreed. "Sure," he said softly. "I'll drop something down, if any of them heads that way. You're probably safe," he added. "They don't look like they're about to move."

Quarters were cramped below deck, but that meant there weren't many places to look. He found the room quickly. Dim light came through a porthole, so he was able to examine the sheets of paper – were they what was called parchment? It was much heavier than paper usually was. Champlain was an impressive artist. The top picture showed a different harbour than the one they were in. It was titled "Le Beau Port."

The pinnace, the kind of boat they were on, was sitting there. On land there were trees and cornfields and groups of people holding their spears aloft. Rivers and streams were sketched in, entering the bay. A few other boats and canoes had been added, along with measurements and a compass indicating direction of the map.

There was another, unfinished, map beside it. Obviously the one Champlain was working on. Jeremy recognized the location of some of the ripened cornfields and where the river entered the bay. This one was labelled "Port Fortune." Not very fortunate, Jeremy thought, for those men who'd been killed.

Judging by the pile of paper sheets, and the many more rolls of it nearby, Champlain had been very busy. Jeremy couldn't help but be impressed by the detail on each map.

He'd better head back up before the funeral service was over and everyone started coming back to the ship.

21.

BACK UP ON DECK, HE WASN'T SURPRISED TO SEE THAT the first boatload of men were starting to climb back on board. He moved back to where he'd left Harv. To his amazement, they bumped. Harv hadn't moved.

"Oh good," Harv said, "you came back up. I was wondering if I should go warn you."

Jeremy looked toward the land. The last of the French had loaded and were firing warning shots at the few men who were now appearing through the trees, even though they were hopelessly out of range.

Champlain and Captain Poutrincourt were coming aboard now, looking grim. Jeremy still had Harv's translator in his hand. He'd been about to give it back, but he wanted to hear what they would say.

"Do you think they'll let our dead be?" the Captain asked.

The other man shook his head. He was pointing ashore. "Look!"

Already some of the men with spears had arrived at the burial spot and started to dig away the sand. Others were pulling down the cross.

"Go! Go!" Poutrincourt commanded. "Fire!"

The last boatload of *arquebusiers* had not quite reached the ship. Other men were scrambling over the rail, returning to the boats.

A few shots were fired from the boats, but they were too far away to hit anyone, as were the arrows that were fired back. By the time the boats reached shore, the natives had fled once more to the safety of the trees.

"It is hopeless to pursue," the captain was saying. "We may have to rebury the men more than once."

"We may have to leave them." Another man was shaking his head. "Perhaps we should have called this place Misfortune."

Jeremy felt his arm caught and tugged back towards the stern of the boat as once again the men ashore were getting back in the boats to return to the ship.

"This could go on forever," Harv was saying. "I think they should just let things be."

Jeremy was surprised. He wondered if "letting things be" was ever a solution. It didn't seem to be in character for Harv. Could it be that he would settle down to be the kind of helpful travelling companion the old Harv was? He seemed to have smartened up a lot just in the few trips they'd taken, and he had shown a practical side by thinking to bring the translator. That reminded Jeremy.

"Here!" he said, fumbling for Harv's hand. "Thanks! That's a super gadget."

"Yeah," Harv added in a whisper, as the ship was becoming more crowded by the rest of the men coming aboard. "It's solved quite a few misunderstandings in my day. Anyway, I've got to get home."

They'd reached the spot they came aboard and Jeremy realized that he was no longer holding Harv's arm. "I've got to go too," he said before he realized he was alone.

It was his turn now. He moved over.

Not a moment too soon. He heard the front door open and voices in the living room. Well, he had expected there'd be company, hadn't he? So there was nothing to do but drag himself out to the kitchen to see if there was anything Mum wanted him to do.

It appeared that Ike was going to barbeque the chops, and Jeremy was enlisted to carry out placemats for the patio table after he'd cleaned it off. Then he had to haul out various condiments, long-handled forks and flippers on a tray, so that he could then stand around and hand things – like some operating-room nurse – to the Great Surgeon Ike, while his mother fluttered back and forth between the kitchen and the backyard with plates and salad bowls, forgetting things and dropping the things she didn't forget. Twitterpated.

He couldn't wait for the meal to be over.

22.

HE KNEW HE WAS BOLTING HIS FOOD. NORMALLY HE'D have stopped and enjoyed the corn on the cob, slurping all the butter he could manage. He liked the baked potato his mother had nuked – again lots of butter. He agreed with Aunt Wendy that baked potatoes were comfort food. And he had to admit that Ike seemed to know how to barbeque a pork chop. But he just wanted to get back to his room so he didn't have to respond to the man's phoney questions.

Luckily, Ike was talking to Mum about something going on at work, so Jeremy was able to tune them out.

That was why his mother had to ask him the question twice. He hadn't realized she was talking to him.

"Jeremy!" She was laughing. "Earth calling Jeremy!" She and Ike were staring at him.

"Sorry," he said. "I guess I was thinking of something else."

"I said," his mother said, looking serious now, "Ike would like to ask you something after supper. Maybe you two could go for a drive..."

She left the idea hanging there, looking hopefully at Jeremy. He wanted to scream and run.

"...maybe go pick up some ice cream for dessert."

Ike was looking at Jeremy. No jolly used-car-salesman look. He looked uncomfortable. Nowhere near as uncomfortable as Jeremy was feeling just now, but he didn't seem to be looking forward to the "talk" either. If Jeremy hadn't been desperately searching for an escape, he'd have felt some sympathy for the man. Jeremy doubted they were supposed to discuss ice cream flavours.

Suddenly the meal had turned to lead in his stomach. Was he going to be sick? He could only hope.

It must have shown in his face. To his surprise, for the first time since he'd come home, his mother went out of twitterpated-mode into mother-mode. There was real concern in her voice. "Jer-Bear! Are you all right?"

He didn't say anything, just clapped his hand over his mouth and made a dash for the house. If she thought he was sick, that was as good as being sick. Anything to avoid a "talk" with Ike.

He'd just made it into the bathroom when he heard the back door. He should have known Mum would be hot on his heels. Quickly he closed the door and locked it, just in case she decided to come in.

It didn't take long before she was knocking on the door. "Jeremy? Are you okay?"

Nothing for it now but to make barfing noises and flush the toilet a couple of times. He turned on the tap and splashed some water around. "I'm fine, Mum," he said in a voice he hoped didn't sound fine at all.

What to do now? His mother would notice that the bathroom didn't smell as if anyone had thrown up. Grabbing a can of air freshener from under the sink, he sprayed everywhere. Then he did it again. And again. The freshener smell was so overpowering nobody would want to go in there for a while, but if he didn't get out soon he really would be sick. He flung open the door and staggered out, pulling it shut behind him.

"Better not go in there for awhile...it's pretty potent."

His conscience bothered him a bit to see how worried Mum looked, but he remembered Charlie's dad saying: "Desperate times call for desperate measures." These were desperate times.

"I think I'll just go to bed," he said weakly, going into his bedroom and collapsing on the bed. "Sorry about going for ice cream with Ike."

"Don't worry about it, Jeremy." Ike's voice. He'd evidently followed them in and was now standing behind Mum in the bedroom doorway. "Your mother and I can go later...if you are all right, that is."

"You're sure you haven't got the flu or something?" Mum was still all concern.

Now that he was safely off the hook for little talks with Ike, he'd better reassure Mum. He didn't want her hovering over him all night. "Actually, I feel a lot better already," he said. Careful, Jer, he thought, don't get too well too soon. He shut his eyes. "Just a bit tired, now...you go ahead and get your ice cream." He said the last bit slowly – drowsily.

He could feel Mum lifting the comforter off the foot of the bed and spreading it over him. "All right," she said.

He heard his door close softly behind them and Ike's voice out in the hall.

"Don't worry Sandy, he probably just ate too fast. He was really shovelling that food in."

Thanks Ike, Jeremy thought. Make me seem like a pig. But he didn't really care. He lay there listening to the sounds of the dishwasher being loaded. Finally a knock on his door.

"We're going...you sure you'll be okay?"

Careful now, must balance between too sick to go and well enough to stay. "Fine, Mum," he said not too weakly he hoped.

He heard the front door open. Ike was probably getting impatient.

"Call me on my cell if you need me," Mum called as she left.

Jeremy heaved a sigh of relief. But the relief didn't last long. He knew he'd just postponed the "talk." And he'd played his sick card. Next time he'd be stuck.

23.

He was staring miserably at the ceiling when the phone rang. Was Mum checking up on him already?

"Hey, kiddo!" Aunt Wendy's voice. "You don't sound too chipper. What's up?"

"Gloom and doom," he said mournfully. "Ike was here for supper...as usual...and Mum decided he and I should go get ice cream or something for dessert so we could have a 'talk.' He was supposed to ask me something." Jeremy let all his misery come through in his voice.

There was a long pause. "Great Horny Toads!" Aunt Wendy's voice was shrill. She sounded as upset as he was. "Sounds like he was supposed to be asking you for her hand in marriage or something!"

That almost made him laugh. Almost. Did people really ask for hands in marriage any more? Could that have been it?

"I didn't go...pretended I was sick to my stomach...so they went without me."

"So you're off the hook," Aunt Wendy's voice was soft, sympathetic, "...for now."

Jeremy nodded. He couldn't trust himself to speak. Finally he managed. "Yeah...for now." Tomorrow night he would be doomed. "Any brilliant advice?"

Another long pause. "Sorry, kiddo. Can't think of anything just now. Hang on...don't give up. All he can do is ask, and you'll just have to say you need time to get used to the idea or something like that. Keep me posted." Aunt Wendy didn't sound very cheerful. "Luckily, your mother isn't the type to elope."

Jeremy said good night. Aunt Wendy hadn't made him feel any better. The idea of eloping hadn't occurred to him before. True, his mother wasn't the impulsive type, but she wasn't behaving normally. Who knew what she'd do? Now he was really depressed.

He had just put on his PJs when he noticed the Instant Messenger light flashing. How long had that been going on?

It had to be Mel. Jeremy hurried over to his desk. Melanie wasn't noted for her patience.

"hi Mel sorry I was delayed," he typed.

"is yur mere still hangin out with jerk?"

Jeremy typed yes and stuck in a gloomy happy face symbol – the one with the down-turned mouth. On second thought he stuck in two more.

"I no I told u 2 be nice 2 him but u better not be 2 nice r mere will think u wud be happy to hav him. 4 sum dum reason meres think u need father & anybode will du."

Jeremy groaned. Two people in a row telling him about the possibility of Ike becoming a permanent fixture in his life – he tried not to think the word "stepfather" but it kept popping up. His stomach was starting to ache again. It wouldn't have been so bad if he didn't know Mel was right. Mum was just the sort to think she was depriving Jeremy of the influence of a man in his life, so even when the twitterpated stuff wore off, she might stick with Ike if she thought it would make Jeremy happy.

"Ya," he typed. "You're right, I have to be careful."

"must go mere wants 'quality time' nite u hang in ther bye"

Hang on! Hang in! Some advice, Jeremy thought grimly. Melanie had just made him feel worse. He hadn't thought about the possibility that being nice to Ike could backfire.

He was doomed no matter what he did. He just wanted to run away.

He picked up the stamp album, then noticed the envelope of stamps Mr. Matthews had sent. He need something different. He didn't care what.

The Australian stamp – the Sydney-Hobart race – must have been a good one if they did a stamp for it.

Wow! That sailboat was really tossing on the waves.

He wondered if it was the boat that won the race. That would be exciting to sail on. He needed something thrilling enough to take his mind off his misery, and he hadn't been in a sailing race since he'd ridden on the *Bluenose I*. That had been exhilarating. Maybe what he needed right now was some suspense.

Anything would be better than feeling the way he did right now. He picked up the stamp and the magnifying glass.

AND LANDED IN THE MIDST of the worst storm he'd ever seen, let alone imagined. Water buried the deck of the boat. He grabbed for a handhold, but his hands slipped away with the next onslaught of water. It was in his mouth, in his face, in his eyes. He couldn't see. Choking and gasping, he could barely catch his breath.

Desperately struggling to breathe, he tried to fight his way back to where he'd come aboard. That was the only way to get back home. But he didn't know where it was. He'd been hit by water and pushed about from the instant he'd arrived.

The yacht he was on was not that big. Maybe ten or eleven metres long. This was a racing yacht, not a fishing boat like the *Bluenose.*

He managed to grab hold of something that felt like a rope. He just hoped it was attached to something sturdy. He could feel himself sliding — the rope wasn't going to hold. But it did, as he slammed into something.

He gulped for air and felt his mouth fill with water.

For a moment he managed to blink the water out of his eyes. What he saw made him wish he hadn't. Waves higher than a six-story building seemed to encircle the boat, ready to crash down on it. Useless to try to duck or dodge them. Two men on deck wearing harnesses and lifelines were trying to remove broken bits of mast that swung crazily about. The crew had managed to strip the craft of all its sails except for the storm jib, but Jeremy couldn't imagine there was any way they'd make it through this gale. Somehow he'd have to drag himself around the deck until he accidentally found his magic entry point. His doorway to get out of this.

He didn't get a chance. He could see a monster wave coming in. It made the house-sized ones look puny. He didn't have a harness and he wasn't going to take any chances being washed overboard. He doubted he could hold on to anything when this one hit. He dived down the hatchway just as it did.

Now he was rolling, tossing, completely under water. Something hit his shoulder. He came up gasping for air. He could see two other men down here with him.

"It's over!" one yelled.

Jeremy realized he didn't mean the storm was over. The boat was upside down. Turned over. The deck was beneath them – completely under water.

24.

"THE CREW HARNESSED ON DECK WILL DROWN," ONE man shouted. He took a deep breath and dove down.

Was he planning on swimming through the hatch to try to rescue them? Jeremy wondered.

He didn't have to wonder for long. He was under water again, trying to hold what little breath he had and not take in any more sea water. Then his head was out of the water.

Somehow the craft had righted itself! He was up to his neck in water but he could see the hatchway above him. Spitting water, he made for it.

He hoped, as he scrambled for the deck, that the sea would be calmer. No such luck! But to his amazement there was a rescue helicopter overhead. Good. If the yacht sank, and he couldn't see how it wouldn't, the men would be saved.

The moment of relief that he'd felt at that thought didn't last. There was no way anybody could rescue him.

He was an invisible stowaway. He'd go down with the boat or be swept into the ocean. Either way he didn't have a chance. He'd drown.

He just had to find the spot he'd come aboard. Maybe it was near that broken spar. He remembered glimpsing it in those first few terrifying seconds. He fought his way over. Huge waves towered all around the boat, seconds away from descending. If only another one didn't hit before he could move around the spar. It was his only chance. Spray lashed at his face as he struggled against the wind.

He was right! Instantly the roar of the storm ceased. He was home.

Jeremy jumped out of his desk chair. His pyjamas were soaked and he was shaking all over, and it wasn't because he was cold! That had been the narrowest escape ever. Dumping his soggy PJs in the plastic wastepaper basket, he dug an old pair of flannelette ones out of his drawer and then decided that he'd put on his robe. Feeling warm and safe again would stop his heart from pounding quite so much.

The important thing was being safe. Safe at home.

He heard the front door open. Mum was home. Thank goodness he was back. She'd be sure to check up on him the minute she came in, and a few minutes ago he was nearly drowning in the Tasman sea. She'd have seen him sitting up in his chair looking as if he was unconscious. He'd never found out what would happen if someone tried to "waken" him when he was time travelling. A couple of times he'd been caught, but he usually looked at the stamps in bed, so it just looked as if he was asleep.

Sure enough, his door opened and his mother poked her head in.

"How are you doing? Feeling better or is your stomach still upset?"

Jeremy just nodded. He knew the knots of tension in his belly were caused by the terrifying adventure he'd just had. He could still feel the cold water slapping his face and taste the salt of the sea water on his lips. He shivered involuntarily.

Mum looked really alarmed now. Before Jeremy could speak she was feeling his forehead. "You're cold as ice! Maybe you're coming down with flu!" She shoved him towards his bed. "I'll get you a hot water bottle."

She turned, almost colliding with Ike in the doorway.

"How's our guy doing?" The hearty TV-used-car-salesman voice was back.

Jeremy hadn't realized Ike had come back with her. Seeing him there added another knot to his stomach. Surely she'd tell the UCS to buzz off now. He crawled into bed and lay there waiting.

"I'll be with you in a minute, Ike." She put her arm around him and pulled him out the door with her.

How many knots can a guy have in his stomach? Jeremy wondered. Obviously Ike was staying.

He didn't even open his eyes when Mum shoved the hot water bottle in at his feet. He couldn't wait to be warm enough to go to sleep and end this terrible, horrible, no good, very bad day.

25.

Jeremy woke up feeling doomed. It took him a minute to figure out why. And then he remembered.

This would definitely not be a good time to make a Good Things/Bad Things list. In fact he couldn't think of a single Good Thing. Except maybe that he had a day to figure out what to do when Ike came by tonight and the inevitable "talk" happened.

He'd almost forgotten the terrifying time in the yacht race. Almost. He crawled out of bed and googled the Sydney-Hobart Yacht Race of 1998. Of the 115 yachts that started, only forty-four made it to the finish. Most managed to limp in or be towed to shore. Fifty-five sailors winched to safety by paramedics in helicopters. Five yachts lost. Six sailors dead. He was lucky to be alive.

So why didn't he feel lucky? Being alive should definitely count as a Good Thing, shouldn't it? He was glad he wasn't still struggling for his life on the other side of the world, but he wished he was somewhere other than here.

The doorbell rang and he heard Ike's voice. Was he picking Mum up for work? Jeremy glanced at the clock. He'd really slept in, it was nearly eleven o'clock! It wasn't a weekday – it was Saturday morning. Mum had told him she'd invited Ike for Saturday brunch. Jeremy groaned. Could he pretend he was still sick?

He was about to crawl back into bed when he heard the bell again. What now? He could hear Mum and Ike talking in the kitchen. Then he heard the door opening and someone calling.

"Hello, people! Anybody home?" He recognized the voice.

Aunt Wendy! What was she doing here? He threw on his robe. Was he imagining things? He had to be sure, see with his own eyes. He made it to the living room just ahead of his mother. It was true. He was not imagining the hug.

"I was going to phone, but I left so early and then I just thought I'd surprise you!" She looked down at Jeremy. "Hey, kiddo! Still hangin' in?" She didn't wait for an answer. "You," she said, reaching out to shake hands, "must be Ike!"

Jeremy tried to analyse the look on his mother's face. Puzzled, of course, but was there some suspicion too? He couldn't tell. She was smiling and giving her sister a hug now. Maybe it had just been the shock of the surprise.

"The reason this is so sudden," Aunt Wendy was explaining, "is that I didn't know I'd be coming until the end of work yesterday. There's a motivational seminar at the Mayfield Inn. Someone else was supposed to go and couldn't at the last minute. So then I had to work late getting the information, rush home and get ready. By that time it was too late to phone."

"What time did you leave?" Jeremy's mother was staring. "It's a six-hour drive."

Aunt Wendy laughed. "I left around five. Not much traffic. I figured it would be better than driving with the Friday night crowd." She sniffed. "Do I smell bacon?"

Mum nearly knocked Jeremy over rushing back to the kitchen. Ike followed her. That left him alone with Aunt Wendy.

"Do you," he whispered, "really have a meeting?"

"I'm going to a couple of sessions this afternoon and tomorrow. But I wasn't exactly chosen to attend. I pushed myself into it. Not that anybody else wanted to go."

He really didn't care. He wasn't sure his stomach could handle brunch after all the shocks it had had. But when his mother dished up the omelette he realized he would be fine. Everything would be fine now that Aunt Wendy was here. He hoped.

"Are you sure you don't want to stay here?" Jeremy's mother was saying when Aunt Wendy explained she was booked into the Mayfield Inn.

They were sitting in the living room. Jeremy had somehow ended up sitting beside Ike across from Aunt Wendy, who'd been talking to him while Jeremy helped his mother bring in the napkins and coffee. It looked to Jeremy as if the "talk" had been mostly questions on Aunt Wendy's side. Like some kind of job interview.

"Have you managed to find a permanent place to stay?" was the last one. Aunt Wendy was smiling as if to offset the bluntness of her question. "I hear there's a real problem finding apartments in Edmonton just now."

Ike was looking around, rather uncomfortably.

Hey, answer the question, it can't be that hard, Jeremy thought. He turned and stared at the man sitting beside him.

Ike started to answer, but Jeremy's mother interrupted him.

"I've been wondering..." she began nervously, "we've been wondering...about fixing up a suite in the base-ment." She looked apologetically at Jeremy. "Ike was going to talk to you about it."

So, Jeremy thought, that was it. He wasn't sure whether foot-in-the-basement was any better than hand-in-marriage. Either way, he'd be stuck with the guy twenty-four/seven.

Luckily, it seemed Jeremy wasn't expected to say

anything just now. Aunt Wendy had taken care of that with questions about zoning laws and building permits.

Apparently, his mother hadn't looked into that. Another sign that she wasn't behaving normally. His mother was the practical one, but now she and Aunt Wendy seemed to have switched roles altogether.

Ike finally managed to say something. "I did look into buying a condo when I first got here," he said, "but the company didn't seem to be sure how long I'd be staying in Edmonton." It wasn't his old used-car-salesman confident voice and he was looking at Jeremy's mother apologetically. "Sorry, Sandy, I guess I didn't tell you."

Obviously he hadn't. Mum was looking completely shocked. "But..." she began, "...I thought..." Then she stopped and stared at Ike Morton.

Jeremy had been on the receiving end of looks like that a few times. Bad report cards. One memorable time in Grade Three when he'd claimed he'd forgotten to bring a bad one home and the teacher had finally phoned to see why his mother hadn't signed it. He was almost starting to feel sorry for Ike.

Ike obviously didn't realize how much trouble he was in. "Now, Sandy," he was saying, "the basement suite was your suggestion."

Oh boy! The man's just getting himself into more trouble. Jeremy got up and went to take some of the coffee cups out to the dishwasher. He was about to pick up Aunt Wendy's but she beat him to it and followed him.

"You could always have rented it to someone else," Ike was saying. "It would have added to the value of the house when you sold it." The used-car-salesman-type pitch seemed to be running down. "You might have wanted to move to Vancouver?" he finished lamely.

Jeremy knew that if anything was being said now they could still hear it from the kitchen. He knew that Ike was getting the silent treatment and "the look." He just stood there in the kitchen watching Aunt Wendy load the dishwasher. Neither of them dared say a word.

Then his mother came down the hallway. "Ike and I are going for a little drive," she said. "We've got some things to sort out." Her voice was softer as she added. "Sorry, Wendy, I know you've got a meeting to attend..."

"It's okay," her sister whispered. "I can skip the afternoon one and go tonight. I'll be here when you get back."

They waited until the front door closed and they heard the Audi drive away.

26.

"Your problem may be solved," Aunt Wendy sighed, "but I fear your mother is going to be even more gun-shy – or should I say guy-shy – than ever. I'm sorry. You were obviously right about the guy being a bit of a phoney though." She poured herself another coffee. "So I guess it'll turn out all right."

"What was she thinking of? A basement suite?" Jeremy shook his head. "He wouldn't have stayed in a basement suite, would he?"

"Ever hear the one about the kind-hearted Arab and the camel?"

Jeremy wasn't sure he wanted to hear a joke just now, but maybe Aunt Wendy thought he need cheering up. "Nope."

"You see, it's really cold in the desert at night, and the poor camel looked so miserable that his owner decided that he'd just let the camel put his nose in the tent." Aunt

Wendy was still loading dishes in the dishwasher.

Jeremy was grinning now. "Ignoring the fact that camels are supposed to have very bad breath?"

"Don't interrupt the story!" Aunt Wendy was trying to give him a mean-teacher look, but she spoiled it by crossing her eyes. "Anyway, next thing the poor man knows, the camel's got his head in, and the man wakes up to find out that it's getting cramped and the camel's stuck his shoulders in and, of course, by morning the kind-hearted man is lying outside in the cold because the camel has climbed completely into the tent and there's no room for both of them."

Jeremy laughed. "So you think Ike would have been a camel who'd start in the basement and take over the whole house?"

"Don't worry." Aunt Wendy reached over and gave him a hug. "I think your mother would have figured it out eventually."

Jeremy was doubtful. She hadn't been behaving like somebody who'd figure something out unless it fell on her. It was the twitterpated thing. He had an idea.

"Was she like this before?" he asked. "I mean when she met Dad?"

Aunt Wendy was thoughtful. "Hmmm...smart kid," she said. "Of course she was only nineteen. And you have to remember, I was the kid sister." She grinned. "She was the oldest, and the sensible one...as our parents would constantly point out!"

She had been wiping that piece of counter for quite a while. Now she stopped completely and just stared at the wall. "It just seemed like a normal romance to me. They met, they dated, they broke up." She turned to Jeremy with a little smile. "Your dad was always late for things and it drove Miss Punctual crazy!"

Jeremy nodded. He could just imagine.

"But they always made up and got back together. And, well, that's how it went then – you dated and then you got married." Aunt Wendy shrugged.

"So she wasn't...ummm...twitterpated?" Jeremy felt a bit let down. It looked like studying history wasn't going to help this time.

"Twitterpated? *Bambi*, right?" Aunt Wendy laughed, wrung out the dishcloth and hung it up. "Well, I guess you might say that she was at first, but she got over it...the being late really bugged her...so after a while it settled down. You know, she saw his faults but decided the good things were more important."

She came over and gave Jeremy a hug. "Anyway, that's how it was at first."

Jeremy felt a bit relieved. With any luck Mum had already started recognizing some of Ike's faults. But what if she decided there were more Good Things than Bad?

27.

THEY WERE SITTING IN THE LIVING ROOM. AUNT WENDY was on her third cup of coffee and Jeremy was having a Coke when Ike's car pulled up in front. He resisted the urge to run to the window.

He heard a car door close. Aunt Wendy looked at him. "Oh, oh! She didn't slam the door!" The another door opened and a few moments later closed just as quietly. She looked puzzled.

"He always does the gentleman thing," Jeremy said, "and opens her door."

Aunt Wendy looked impressed. "Well," she said, "he can't be all bad!"

Footsteps were coming up the walk, but Jeremy couldn't tell it if was one person or two. Had he heard another door close? He wasn't sure. No. There were voices on the front step. He looked miserably at Aunt Wendy. Then the front door opened and Mum came in. Alone.

Jeremy resisted the impulse to smile. He'd let Aunt Wendy handle things. She didn't get a chance.

"Well," said his mother. "I think that's sorted out."

Even though he'd had eleven years of experience, Jeremy was having trouble reading her expression. He thought he knew them all, but this was different from anything he'd seen before.

Aunt Wendy seemed to think she knew. Her voice was all sympathy. "You okay?"

His mother smiled, but it wasn't a real smile. Jeremy couldn't interpret it either. Definitely not happy. Kind of tired, but not hopeless.

"I'm fine!" she said. In Jeremy's opinion she looked anything but.

"So," he said trying not to sound too scared, "what's sorted out?"

His voice must have betrayed him anyway because his mother gave him a funny, apologetic look. He guessed it was supposed to be a smile, but it fell apart at the corners.

"Sorry, Jer-Bear," she said. "I know you like Ike...but I guess the basement thing was a shocker...I mean when you'd barely met the man."

Jeremy hoped his mother hadn't caught the wide-eyed look Aunt Wendy was giving him. It was hard enough not to let his own amazement show. He'd have to tell Mel that he'd succeeded in carrying out her advice – without even trying.

"So I take it the basement suite thing is off?" Aunt

Wendy asked. Jeremy thought she was being very brave. It was a question he wouldn't have dared ask.

Mum nodded. "I guess I rushed into that," she said. "Ike explained that I was so excited about the idea that he hadn't the heart to disappoint me." She turned to Jeremy. "He was going to ask your advice on how to break the news when you two went for the drive." She had the funny, sad look on her face again. "He thought you might be able to help him...as he put it...'let me down easy.'"

This time Jeremy was pretty sure he couldn't help looking shocked. Could it be Ike wasn't so bad? Luckily, Mum was looking at Aunt Wendy.

"Are you sure you don't want to stay here?" It sounded more like a plea than a question. "Just for tonight?"

To Jeremy's relief his aunt nodded. It would be good to have her stay overnight, just in case Mum was more upset than she let on.

"I left in such a hurry, I didn't have time to make a reservation, so it's not a problem." She winked at Jeremy.

She probably planned to stay here all along, he realized, grinning. "You can have my bed," he offered happily. "I'll sleep on the couch."

"Why don't you bunk with me?" His mother was looking happier. "We can talk half the night, like we used to when we slept together growing up."

"Great!" Aunt Wendy laughed, "and I can eat potato chips in bed and drive you crazy just like I used to!"

Even Mum was laughing now. Everything was going

to be okay. Maybe Ike wasn't gone forever, but Jeremy had learned a thing or two. About hanging on and hanging in and how it helped to have people to talk to.

He'd leave Mum and Aunt Wendy to talk. He was going to write to Mel.

In his room he spotted his wet PJs in the wastepaper basket. Better get those down to the dryer before Mum found them and wanted an explanation. He picked them up.

For a moment he could hear the roar of the storm, feel the salt water against his face and know the terror.

The really important thing, he decided, was surviving. He could do that just fine.

BIBLIOGRAPHY

Armstrong, Joe C.W. *Champlain.* Toronto: Macmillan Canada, 1987.

Cartier, Jacques. *The Voyages Of Jacques Cartier.* Introduction by Ramsay Cook. Toronto: University of Toronto Press, 1993

Darnell, Emanuel and Rousseau, Lyse. *Darnell Millennium Stamps Of Canada Catalogue.* Montreal: Darnell Publishing, 2000.

Dionne, N.E. *Champlain.* University Of Toronto Press, 1963.

Donaldson-Forbes, Jeff. *Jacques Cartier.* New York: Rosen Pub., 2002

Hudak, Heather C. *Jacques Cartier.* Calgary: Weigl Educational Publishers, 2005.

Morison, Samuel Eliot. *Samuel De Champlain*. Boston: Atlantic Monthly Press Book, Little Brown & Company,1972.

Mundle, Rob. *Fatal Storm: The Inside Story Of The Tragic Sydney-Hobart Race*. Camden, Me.: International Marine/McGraw Hill, 1999.

Santella, Andrew. *Jacques Cartier*. Chicago: Heinemann, 2002.

Scott Specialized Catalogue Of Canadian Stamps. Toronto: Unitrade Press, 1989.

Toye, William. *The St. Lawrence*. Toronto: Oxford University Press, 1959.

Wade, Mason. *The French Canadians, Vol. 1: 1760–1967*. Toronto: Macmillan Canada, 1955.

ABOUT THE AUTHOR

O ne of Canada's best-known children's authors, Cora Taylor has published nearly a dozen juvenile novels, including *Ghost Voyages, Ghost Voyages II: The Matthew,* and *The Deadly Dance* for Coteau; *On Wings of a Dragon, Angelique: Buffalo Hunt,* and others. She has received numerous awards and commendations for her work, and has served in writer-in-residence positions from St. Albert, Alberta, to Tasmania.

Cora Taylor was born in Fort Qu'Appelle, Saskatchewan, and grew up on a farm near Fort Carlton. After moving to Alberta in the 1950s, she studied writing with W.O. Mitchell, Rudy Wiebe and others. Her first book, *Julie,* was published in 1985. Cora currently divides her time between Edmonton, Ontario, and Florida.